# REBIRTH

SKYE MALONE

Rebirth
Book Six of the Awakened Fate Series



Cover design by Karri Klawiter
www.artbykarri.com

ISBN-10: 1-940617-55-3
ISBN-13: 978-1-940617-55-8

Library of Congress Control Number: 2016906815

**Join Skye Malone's mailing list to hear about new releases!**
**www.skyemalone.com/mailinglist**

# PRONUNCIATION GUIDE

**Dehaian** (deh-HYE-an)
**Greliaran** (greh-lee-AR-an)
**Nyciena** (ny-SEE-en-uh)
**Ruanir** (ru-ahn-eer)
**Strakirin** (strah-KEE-rehn)
**Teariad** (tee-AR-ee-ad)
**Tiberion** (ty-BEE-ree-un)
**Yvaria** (ih-VAR-ee-uh)

# 1

## ARI

Sometimes I wonder if everything in my life might have been simpler if I'd never met him.

I mean, not *simpler,* exactly. Nothing in my life has ever been simple, not even back then. And besides, if he hadn't shown up, I probably would have died.

But sometimes… just sometimes… I wonder what might've been. What my life would look like if I'd stayed home from the party that night. What could have happened if I'd simply refused to attend. Maybe my whole world might not have changed. All the secrets around me might have stayed hidden.

If not for that one moment.

The moment I met Noah Delaney.

"So honestly, what *do* you think of this dress?"

I blinked, pulling my gaze from the cool summer night beyond the gazebo archways. In a red gown so tight she'd probably been sewn into it, my mother waited for my response.

"It looks great," I managed, knowing she expected the answer no matter what I actually thought.

She tossed a lock of her golden-brown hair over her shoulder, using the motion to cover a surreptitious glance to the crowd. "Good." Her perfectly painted mouth pursed in consideration. "Get some drinks, would you?"

I paused, debating whether to point out that I was seventeen, but I knew it wouldn't do any good. It was a hollow argument anyway, especially here. Most of the people around me were well over a hundred and fifty, and couldn't care less for human laws about alcohol.

"Sure."

She ignored the response, her focus still on the room.

I walked toward the bar on the opposite side of the massive gazebo. Tall tables dotted the space, providing a spot for people to leave their drinks or cluster around for conversation. Clouds of perfume and heavy cologne hit me as I wove through the crowd. The air was stuffy despite the open archways around the walls, and the flowering vines twisting across the ceiling just added to the haze. Snatches of conversation flitted past me, nonsensical.

I hated events like this.

"Two glasses of the house red, please," I said to the bartender when he glanced my way.

He didn't bother to ask for an ID. While he turned to get the wine, I leaned against the white marble of the bar and watched the party.

The sooner we could get back to Chicago, the happier I'd be. I wasn't much for crowds, though my mother loved them, and schmoozing with people in a gazebo outside Judge Engle's mansion was worlds away from my idea of a good time. At this point, I'd have paid money to be curled up in bed with a book.

"When do you think we can get out of here without causing a fuss?" came an idle comment to my right.

I glanced over as my cousin Maia leaned back against the bar. Her long brown hair was twisted up in an ornate arrangement of braids and glistening rhinestone accents, and her blue dress matched the dark color of her eyes. By her side, her girlfriend Dhanya looked gorgeous with her deep green dress setting off her olive skin and black hair. With a raised eyebrow, Maia regarded me while Dhanya tried to catch the bartender's attention.

A smile tweaked my lip. "Is *now* too soon?"

Maia grinned. "Where's Jace?"

"Back at the hotel."

"Traitor," Dhanya commented with her customary dry humor.

I chuckled. "Adjustment."

Understanding replaced the amusement in their eyes and brought with it a strong dash of sympathy. They'd both been through it a year before.

"Let us know if he needs anything," Dhanya offered, her dry tone gone.

I nodded. I felt bad for my older brother. Yes, he'd missed this, for which I envied him, but he was also dealing with the side effects of the adjustment, for which I really didn't. It'd hit him later than normal—most ruanir experienced the reaction to magic that extended our lives at about eighteen or nineteen, and Jace was already twenty—and he'd spent the better part of the past week under a doctor's care, looking like hell all the while.

I might've taken that over this party, however, and I wasn't sure he wouldn't agree—to the point where I wondered if he wasn't playing it up a bit.

Guilt colored the thought. Jace wouldn't leave me alone with Mom if he could help it. He knew what she was like.

The bartender set the glasses of wine next to me.

"Thanks," I said.

He nodded, but his attention was already on the next person calling out a drink order. I scanned the room for Mom and found her fawning over one of Judge Engle's assistants.

She worked fast, my mother.

I sighed, leaving the drinks where they were. I was familiar with how she operated. Assistant to a judge or not, she'd want to give the man a chance to order her a drink first. Asking me to come over here had probably just been a ruse to get me out of the way. I should've picked up on it sooner. In the three years since Dad had died and Jace and I had moved in with Mom, I'd had ample opportunity to learn her patterns.

"So have you told her?" Dhanya asked Maia.

Her voice tugged me from the dark turn my thoughts were taking. I glanced back to them both, my eyebrow rising with curiosity. "Told me what?"

Maia blushed. She pulled her hand out from where it had braced her on the bar.

My mouth fell open with surprise. A large diamond glinted on Maia's left ring finger, the stone set beautifully with princess-cut sapphires around it, all on a platinum band.

"Dhanya asked me last night," Maia said.

I managed to get my mouth shut, though words still failed me. "Maia... I..." A laugh escaped me. I threw my arms around her.

Maia laughed as well, squeezing me back. After a heartbeat, I let her go and hugged Dhanya.

"I want to hear everything," I told them.

"She asked me at that restaurant downtown," Maia said. "The one where we had our first date. She even had a violinist play the first song we ever danced to."

I grinned approvingly.

"I was *so* scared she'd say no," Dhanya added.

"Why?" Maia replied, incredulous.

Dhanya shrugged.

Maia put her arm around Dhanya and gave her a quick kiss. "Silly. You never had a single thing to worry about."

I smiled. I loved how much they cared about each other. Maia was one of my favorite people in the world, and she deserved someone who treated her as well as Dhanya did.

"I totally want you to be my maid of honor," Maia continued to me. "Is that alright?"

"Of course! Thank you!"

"Great. We're thinking next May."

"Sounds wonderful."

She smiled.

I caught sight of my mother looking my direction, her eyebrow raised. Judge Engle's assistant was walking away, his head bowed in deep conversation with another man, and both men were leaving the room.

Mom didn't look happy in the least. I kept myself from grimacing.

Maia sighed and when I glanced back, I could see she'd spotted my mother's expression. "We'll talk more later," she assured me.

"Sorry."

She shook her head dismissively.

I picked up the drinks. "Later," I promised them both.

They smiled. I headed back toward Mom.

She snatched the wine from me the moment I came near, annoyance clear in her every motion. I didn't say anything. It wouldn't help and she'd only take out her frustration on me.

I wished Jace was here.

Stifling a sigh, I took a sip of wine while I watched Mom from the corner of my eye. A socialite to her core, my mother saw her life's work as rectifying the mistakes of the men in her life and finding a way into the social position she so craved—preferably with as low a cost to herself as possible. The judges were her obvious targets. As the leaders of our people, the judges were both feared and admired. In ruanir society, there was no level higher.

She'd had a good start. She'd been the daughter of a judge,

though her mother had lost her position to a scandal when Mom was a teenager. Mom rebounded, though. She would *never* have made the sacrifice to become a judge herself, but with how she'd managed to arrange her own life, there shouldn't have been any need. She'd married my father—a man with a long lineage of judges behind him and a brother who'd become one besides. It should have ended her up with a social standing so high, it would've made her nose bleed.

But then Dad decided he'd never wanted the job. He'd been trained for it, spent his life knowing the day would come to accept the position of it, but when that time arrived… he couldn't. He'd loved people, and art, and he'd made friends wherever he'd gone. To become a judge would have meant giving up all of that—turning cold and emotionless inside, and leaving behind his family, his children, and everything else that he'd once loved for the sake of serving the ruanir. And while Mom didn't care if he had to make that sacrifice—not if it elevated her socially—he did.

So he'd turned his back on all of it. Despite Mom's attempts to cajole him into following that path, he'd chosen to stay with us and pursue his creative passions instead.

Mom had raged. I didn't remember the arguments, but Jace said they had been terrible, and by the time I was three, the whole thing was over. Mom had given up and divorced Dad, leaving us to his care while she ventured off to find another way into high society. It'd taken her well over a decade of scrambling for any scrap of notice the judges threw her way before she'd regained their favor and, in the past year, she'd finally been able to attain that stature she'd so desperately craved. Now she devoted her time to flitting between their numerous parties and distancing herself from any hint that she'd ever been married to my father.

It made me wonder why she'd insisted I come along tonight at all.

Mom straightened, her irritation vanishing into an expression of saccharine friendliness at the same moment that I felt an arm slip possessively around my shoulders.

"Well, Ariabella Moreau," came a smooth voice. "It's been too long."

Adrenaline surged through me, triggering a fight-or-flight impulse so powerful it was all I could do not to lash out. No way. Not him. She wouldn't…

"Logan, so glad you could finally join us," Mom simpered. She had.

"And how are you this evening, Madam Corvienne?" Logan asked.

"Oh, excellent as always," Mom replied. "Ariabella and I were just talking about you."

I made myself keep breathing, ignoring the bald-faced lie. By now, I was used to them.

"Let go of me," I growled to Logan. "Now."

"Ariabella!" Mom reprimanded me.

"It's no problem," Logan said, stepping away from me and holding up his hands. His dark eyes held a look so wry, it felt poisonous. "I know all about Ari's little issue with being touched."

I could see the anger begin simmering behind Mom's pleasant expression, all of it directed at me. I had no issue with being touched. I had every issue in the world with being touched by *him*.

Not that she gave a damn. She'd set me up with him, insisted I go out with him, and even after what happened, her opinion hadn't changed. She didn't believe me when I told her what he'd tried. What I'd barely stopped him from doing. His family was incredibly powerful, after all. His mother was one of the highest-ranking judges in the Judiciary. And to an outside observer, Logan Marseilles' dark hair, smoldering gaze, and male-model build made him look like the type of guy who girls pasted pictures of all over their walls. So people like *him* didn't do things like *that*.

I must have been lying just to spite her.

"We were saying how nice it would be if you could come by our hotel," Mom pressed on, her tone a bit sharper than before, as if daring me to contradict her. "We have to be heading back to Chicago tomorrow, but I know Ariabella would *love* to see you before we go."

I choked and set down the wine glass. "Actually, I—"

"It would be my pleasure."

"Wonderful," Mom said. "Would tomorrow morning work for you?"

"Absolutely."

I was going to be sick. "Excuse me."

"Ariabella," Mom snapped. "Don't be rude to—"

I bolted for the nearest archway, not letting her finish, and

I hoped with everything I had that Logan wouldn't come after me.

I didn't want to be responsible for what I'd do if he did.

The golden glow from the gazebo fell behind me and then the lights of Judge Engle's mansion did too. Pushing past the gate of the fence surrounding the yard, I raced out onto the rocks and scrub grass. Hillocks and small ditches threatened to trip my sandaled feet, but I kept going till the bushes and boulders of the rugged Maine coast hid me from view.

My feet slowed. A shiver ran through me, only partly the fault of the cool night. I should have grabbed the shawl I'd left hanging on a chair.

I shouldn't have come here.

Taking a breath, I sank down onto a rock, the bush behind me sheltering me from the view of anyone who tried to follow. My fingers toyed with the ring on my hand, turning it around and around out of habit while the energy trapped inside it made the green-black gemstone shimmer more than the darkness should have allowed. In the distance, I could see the ocean waves rolling into the shore. I was too close to them, really. The magic pouring off of them was toxic on a good day.

But moving would only bring me back toward the party again.

I couldn't believe her. I couldn't believe she'd try to make me be around him. Mothers were supposed to care about this sort of thing. They were supposed to be horrified and call the enforcers and grab kitchen knives just to keep guys like Logan away.

Instead of inviting back the boy who'd tried to rape her daughter.

The shivers grew stronger. I'd stopped him. I'd destroyed two pieces of my favorite jewelry by using that much magic that quickly and I'd needed a week to fully recover from the output, but that was nothing. Not compared to what could have happened.

I shifted my shoulders against my skin crawling. Jace had wanted to kill him. Probably would, if he saw the guy again. Maia and Dhanya didn't know, though I had no doubt that they'd be right there with Jace if they ever learned of it.

And Mom…

Mom didn't believe me. She thought I was being 'excitable'. She thought he couldn't *possibly* have attempted what I said and that—if I wasn't lying simply to spite her—I was being naïve. I hadn't dated many guys, after all. I *obviously* didn't know what someone being attracted to me looked like.

And so she invited him over again. She pushed me back toward him. She didn't see the way he just liked how desperate she was. How he enjoyed it—the fact she fawned over him when he came around, the fact I hated him and couldn't do anything about it. She only saw visions of marrying me off to that sociopathic bastard, and how it would grant her access to all sorts of powerful people with influence like in her wildest dreams.

Sometimes I hated her so much I thought I'd die from the pressure of it.

A cold wind blew in from the ocean, cutting straight

through my emerald dress despite the fact it was supposed to be summer. Chafing my bare arms, I looked out at the night. I couldn't hear the party anymore; the gazebo was too distant and the rush of wind drown its noise. Scrub grass and sand extended from here to the beach like a mottled cloth of shadows beneath the hair-thin sliver of moon. Black waves swept into the shore, their tumbling foam glistening in what starlight managed to make it past the hazy clouds, while farther out, the water disappeared into the black sky. Like all the judges, Judge Engle lived closer to the ocean than any of us—a stalwart soldier keeping watch on an old and wounded enemy in case it found the strength to fight again.

Because we knew maybe, just *maybe*, that someday it would.

I looked away. It was beautiful. I couldn't deny that. The rush of the waves, the sense of depth just there—*right there*—waiting like a whole world barely beyond your fingertips. I understood what humans and the rest saw in it, I really did.

But it had nothing on Arizona.

On home.

A sigh escaped me. I missed the desert so much it hurt. I missed the way the sun set over the mountains, bright like gold and fire. I missed the way the dry air made you feel like you could see with hawk-eyed detail for miles. I missed the saguaros and the cholla forests and just… just *everything*. I'd had friends there, and a regular school too, rather than the highly exclusive prep school Mom insisted I attend now. I'd lived in an ordinary house, not some high-end condo that mostly felt like a prison. We'd never been normal, Jace and I, but with all of that supporting us, at least we could blend.

I'd lost touch with all of my old friends over these past three years. It was harder now. Dad's world had never really revolved around the ruanir.

Mom's world reminded me of how different we were every day.

I rubbed my arms again, trying to push the maudlin thoughts aside. It didn't matter. I'd get back to the hotel, back to Jace, and when I turned eighteen, I'd move in with him. Sure, a few months ago Mom had tried to stop me from doing exactly that, but that was just her attempt to avoid notice by the human authorities. She wouldn't stop me again.

A shape moved in the shadows at the corner of my eye.

My breath caught and my gaze snapped toward the motion. Large, scraggly bushes met my eyes, the green shapes almost black in the darkness. The wind shifted the branches, and my brow drew down at the sight. I'd seen something else, though. At least, I thought I had.

Something slammed into me, driving me backward off of the rock. Branches snapped on the bush behind me as I fell into it, but the weight shoving at me didn't leave.

A hand clamped over my mouth. A figure held me down— big and heavy and almost certainly male, although his face was lost in the shadows and his body was a black shape in the night. An armband wrapped his muscular bicep, the black fabric stitched with glistening blue threads that picked out the shape of a mountain. Brambles stabbed into my back when he pressed me down. I shouted behind his hand, struggling to break free.

But he was strong. *So* strong. His other arm rose as if to hit me. I gasped, instinctively drawing on the magic stored in my ring, cursing how it was always so slow.

Long blades like translucent knives grew from the back of his forearm.

My eyes went wide. A dehaian. One of those spiky-armed mermaid creatures that never, *ever* bothered us because they didn't even know we *existed*.

He swung the blades at me. My magic couldn't respond fast enough.

Another shape crashed into him, driving him off of me and sending him tumbling away.

My skin stung like I'd suddenly dipped myself in a mild acid. Hissing with pain, I looked toward what had hit him.

A guy stood on the sand. Blond-haired and tall, he had the look of a well-built surfer and he appeared only a year or two older than me. His hands were clenched into fists and muscles stood out from his arms. He scanned the beach with a predatory glare.

And then he turned back to me.

"You okay?" he asked, a wary sort of concern tingeing the words.

I nodded. The acid-burn pain was fading, whatever it'd been. Not taking my eyes from him, I struggled to push to my feet amid the branches and rocks.

He hesitated and then reached out a hand. I took it.

His skin was cold as ice. My brow rose in alarm at the feeling.

He pulled me up and then let go the moment I'd reached my feet.

I swallowed hard. "Who—"

More dark shapes shot past at the corner of my eye. I spun.

They were racing up the beach, heading for the manor. They were moving faster than I'd ever seen anyone run.

And then the screaming started.

I took off. The rocks slowed me and so did the darkness, but when I rounded the bushes, horror was what brought me to a halt.

Scattered tables and chairs. People running into the night. Dark forms chasing them.

Bodies on the ground.

I couldn't tell if they were dead or who they were. In the glare of the gazebo lights and the pitch-black night, details were hard to see.

But it wouldn't be Maia. Or Dhanya or Mom. It just wouldn't. They'd be running away from this. They'd be fine.

Another person dashed from the gazebo. Something sent them lurching forward like they'd been shot and then they were on the ground, impossible vines rushing over their body to pin them down.

A dehaian darted past. The blades on their arm swung down. The person screamed, the sound cutting off with a nauseating gurgle.

The dehaian kept going, racing toward the next person trying to flee.

Energy rushed up inside me, already primed from the other

attack and finally answering my call. The power stored in my ring joined it, adding to its strength, while terror drove a surge from me equal to anything I'd sent at Logan that day.

Magic growled through the ground. Beneath the dehaians' feet, the dirt became like Hollywood quicksand, dragging them down. Roots and vines from the garden tangled around them, fighting their attempts to keep moving.

The last of my magic poured out.

I staggered, my legs weakening, and I dropped to my knees on the rocks. That much energy leaving all at once… it made me feel like a dying man in the Sahara.

The ground rumbled again, more magic tearing through it in waves, originating from closer to the mansion. Hope rose in me. The ruanir were alive. They were fighting back.

A wind kicked up, throwing sand and grit into the air, obscuring everything. Dehaian figures tumbled to the ground, knocked over by the gusts. Others skidded to a stop, looking around frantically; all I could see were their silhouettes and their bloodied spikes in the hazy light from the gazebo. For a moment, the dehaians seemed to debate whether to continue chasing down my people, and then one of them shouted something in a language I'd never heard. As a group, they turned and ran for the water.

Straight toward me.

I gasped, struggling to reach my feet. The dehaians charged at me. I saw the closest take aim with something that looked like a gun.

A cold hand grabbed my arm and yanked me out of the way.

A brown pod struck the place where I'd been. Vines exploded over the ground.

"Run!" the blond guy yelled.

Releasing my arm, he shoved me ahead of him. We took off across the rocks.

The dehaians shouted behind us. I threw a glance back to see half a dozen of them break away from the main group and race after us.

They were so fast.

I stifled a panicked cry. My legs felt thick from the expenditure of magic and I couldn't summon more energy no matter how hard I tried. The sand dragged at my sandals, making me struggle like I had weights attached to my feet.

The boy swore, desperately, vehemently.

Something hit me from behind. The beach disappeared and the night did too. The world became a blanket of fog and a sense of motion surrounded me, like suddenly I was moving with impossible speed.

And it hurt. All of it hurt. Every inch of my skin felt like it was burning.

I shrieked.

The sense of motion shifted instantly. The fog vanished.

I tumbled to the ground, choking on pain even more than shock. I felt like my skin was boiling on my body. I wanted to scream.

I couldn't even breathe.

The agony began to fade. I opened my eyes and looked down at my arms, terrified of what I'd find.

My skin looked normal. Untouched. And meanwhile, the excruciating pain was disappearing like it'd never happened.

But my ring was destroyed. A blackened hole was all that was left of the gemstone in its setting.

I stared. Magic. That'd been magic. An ungodly amount of it that, from the way it'd hurt, *had* to have been from the ocean.

My eyes caught on the scrub grass beneath my hands, and the pale sand as well. My heart pounding, I lifted my gaze. Nothing around me looked like Judge Engle's property. It didn't look like anywhere I remembered seeing at all.

*Definitely* ocean magic.

I shivered, fear running through me. I was okay, though. I wouldn't have absorbed any of it. I just *wouldn't* have. And my ring had probably been destroyed in the fight and I simply hadn't noticed. But meanwhile, I was on a beach that wasn't a thing like the one in Maine. Dunes topped by pale grass shone in the moonlight. The clouds were gone. Even the air was ever-so-slightly warmer than it had been.

The blond guy stood about ten feet away, watching me. "Are you alright?"

His voice was tense. Guarded. He seemed on the edge of leaving.

And he'd brought me here. I wasn't stupid. If it'd been anything else, he'd seem shocked. Or at least he'd be looking around.

He wasn't taking his eyes off me.

My shivering grew stronger. "What are you?"

He hesitated. "What are you?"

I didn't answer. We never told. We hid because that's how we stayed alive. How we prevented witch hunts, kept out of laboratories, and stopped the world from knowing we were real.

Because humans were notoriously bad at tolerating things that were different than them. More powerful than them.

But then, he obviously wasn't human.

I shoved the thought aside. "You first."

"I saved your life."

I was silent. That didn't mean he wasn't a threat.

Without looking away from him, I spread my fingers a bit wider in the sand and focused on the power I could sense there. It was faint—it was *always* so faint—and this close to the ocean it was dangerous as hell. But slowly, I felt magic from the land around me creeping into my skin. After a blast like I'd sent out, it could take weeks before I was back to full strength.

But it didn't matter. I wasn't going to stay defenseless. Not with whatever this guy was around.

His gaze flicked down toward my hands. I tensed. He'd noticed.

"Your ring. It had magic in it, didn't it?"

I stopped breathing.

"I've only seen somebody use jewelry like that once before. A wizard. Joseph." The guy paused. "He wasn't the same as you."

Chills coursed through me. There was no way he could know about Joseph—the crazy, old turtle-man who lived on the coast on the other side of the country and who'd given up on staying in contact with the rest of the ruanir centuries ago. *Nobody* knew about Joseph except us and that group of land-walkers who called themselves the elders.

And this guy definitely wasn't one of *them*.

I tried to push to my feet. My legs still shook, but with the energy trickling in from beneath me, I managed to stand.

The guy retreated a step, a weird expression on his face, almost like he was afraid.

But somehow I suspected that whatever worried him, it wasn't me.

"Are you like him?" he asked. "A wizard?"

I didn't respond.

Anger flared in his eyes. "*Are* you?"

The air stung on my skin. I winced.

That weird, worried look flashed over his face again.

My heart pounded harder. He'd done that. Caused that and he knew it.

A string of swear words rushed through my mind, all of them laced with fear. "No, I'm not like him."

His eyes narrowed as if he'd heard my careful phrasing. "What are you, then?"

I attempted to draw in the magic faster. It wouldn't be enough to hurt him. It'd barely be enough to slow a half-dead sloth. But still.

"Why do you want to know?" I asked.

He paused. "I'm trying to figure out why those dehaians would be trying to kill you."

So he'd heard of dehaians. Okay. And my kind—Joseph at

least.

"What *are* you?" I pressed.

He was silent for a moment. "There isn't a word for what I am. Not anymore."

My brow flickered down. "What does that mean?"

"What I said."

He was infuriating. And dangerous. And this was getting me nowhere. I needed to go back. Dehaians had tried to kill me. *Had* killed people at that party.

My stomach twisted. Maia and Dhanya would be okay, though. Mom too. They'd all be fine.

"Look," I tried. "I don't know what's going on here, but I need to leave. My…" The twisting grew worse. "My family was back there. I need to know if they're alright."

He hesitated.

"Where are we?" I pressed.

"Massachusetts. Roughly."

My eyebrows rose. Roughly in Massachusetts. He said it like he wasn't even sure. And as for how we'd made it a hundred miles…

"How did you do that?"

No response. My annoyance grew.

"Listen," I said. "You're not human. I get that. Witness how I'm not panicking about it. So please just tell me what's going on."

"They were going to kill you. I didn't want to watch someone die in front of me."

I paused. "Thank you."

He nodded, still looking cagy.

"And the rest of it?"

He hesitated. "Hard to explain."

"Try."

"Are you a wizard?"

I swallowed. If he'd wanted to hurt me…

He still could. And we never told. *Never*. There weren't many crimes worse than being someone who told.

But maybe it was a bit late to play human. Maybe I was running out of time to make sure my family was okay.

"We call ourselves ruanir, but… yeah."

I shivered, barely breathing while I waited to see what he would do.

"You don't feel like—" He cut off. "You don't look like Joseph."

My brow drew down. *Feel* like? What did *that* mean? "He's not like us. He chose a different way to live." I waited. "What are you?"

For a moment, he was quiet. "I was a greliaran."

The words were as careful as mine had been, but that didn't stop my surprise. A greliaran. Those creatures my people had made centuries ago to fight the dehaians. They were vicious. Violent and psychotic as serial killers. They transformed into monsters with fire in their skin and in the years after the dehaian war, the judges had left them to go wild. These days, they lived in isolation on the coasts, driven near to madness by their instinctive need to kill dehaians.

And they didn't do a single thing like what I'd seen from

him.

His exact words registered. "*Was?*" I repeated.

"How are your people still alive? I thought Joseph was the only one, because of that… *thing* he did to himself."

My gaze twitched around the beach while I searched for a response. "We found a different way to survive. We forced ourselves to use magic from the land rather than the ocean. It changed us, but not like him." I paused. "How do you even know about us?"

"It's complicated."

"You were a greliaran. I didn't think they knew my people still existed."

"They don't."

"Could you give me a straight answer please?"

He grimaced. "I know about Joseph because I met him. I was there when he died."

I blinked. Joseph was dead?

"And the rest is a long story," he finished. "I don't really want to get into it."

"What about this? How could you get us all the way here?"

He watched me and for the longest moment, the waves on the beach were the only sound. "Because I'm only part greliaran. I'm also a creature called the Beast."

My lungs stopped working. That wasn't possible. That just…

No. *Please* no. He couldn't be the *Beast,* the monster that had hunted us nearly to extinction and that haunted the nightmares of every child of my people. That creature was gone. We'd survived it. Found a way to hide from it till it disappeared.

We'd changed ourselves to take in magic from the land rather than the ocean, even though it wasn't nearly as strong, nearly as dependable. It'd been our only choice, short of hiding in a bubble of protection and never leaving as Joseph had done. The magical energy coming from us had been the signal that monster had used to track us down and, by changing like we had, we'd altered that signal too.

*Feel* like Joseph, he'd said. I shivered. Oh God.

But my ancestors' stories spoke of the Beast. They said it was a storm, but with a mind. A hurricane that could think, that could vanish in a heartbeat, that could shake the ground and rip whole cities down in its wake. A merciless, amorphous predator that made the greliarans my people had created seem like little baby bunny rabbits by comparison.

No one said a word about it being able to look like a *human*.

I backpedaled, my legs answering fear where they wouldn't anything else.

"I'm not going to hurt you," he called.

My sandals caught on a rock, tripping me. I dropped to the sand.

"I *won't*," he insisted. "I'm not a threat to you."

"Did you kill Joseph?"

He paused. "No."

The word was careful. I eyed him, not trusting it.

"The Beast was there, but I didn't kill him," he continued. "Other greliarans attacked him. They weren't with me. Either part of me."

"Why were you at Judge Engle's mansion tonight? Were you

looking for us?”

“No.”

“Then why were you *there*?” I barely kept from shouting.

“I was just passing by. I saw the dehaians coming out of the water. I saw one of them attack you.”

My brow furrowed. “But they were dehaians.” At his blank expression, I continued. “They’re like… they made you.”

“I don’t work for them.”

He said it so plainly, I almost laughed. Their attack dog, their thunderstorm from hell… didn’t work for them.

“I’m not a threat to you,” he persisted. “But if you really don’t know why those dehaians attacked you…” He grimaced. “They were Yvarian. I need to figure out why they’d do that.”

“What’s an Yvarian?”

“A country. Or the dehaians from it. They shouldn’t be doing this without a good reason.”

“And you know this how?”

He hesitated. “I know them. Their king and his…” Another weird expression, this one unreadable. “Girlfriend.”

I studied him warily. “You know their king, but you don’t work for them?”

“Yes.”

The word was emphatic. It felt like there was a *lot* more behind it.

I pushed the thought aside. None of this mattered.

“I need to get back,” I said.

I needed to warn everyone that the Beast had returned.

And that it looked like an attractive guy anybody could

mistake for a human on the street.

The shivers weren't stopping.

He nodded. "Yeah." He hesitated. "It hurt you, though. What I did. Didn't it?"

I tensed. My shoulder rose and fell in a lopsided shrug, though the motion didn't even come close to the truth. Ocean magic in close proximity; I hadn't felt anything that excruciating in my life.

"I'm sorry."

My brow twitched lower.

"If you call someone, can they come get you?"

"I think so."

If they were still alive.

I stuffed the thought down quickly. They'd be fine. They'd *all* be fine.

His gaze flicked over my emerald dress and I knew what he saw. The dress was destroyed. Dirt and sand smudged the silken fabric and I could feel the cool night air through tears on the back where branches had ripped through.

It was certain to raise questions.

He glanced around at the empty beach. "Okay, then, um… let's find you a phone."

I tensed all over again. He was coming with me? That couldn't be good. Yes, he'd saved my life, and no, he hadn't killed any of us earlier tonight, but that didn't mean he wouldn't try later.

It didn't mean anything at all.

He started toward a wooden walkway that led from the beach and then paused when I didn't follow. "You coming?"

I couldn't do anything about it. Not right now. I didn't have enough magic inside me to rattle a teacup, let alone take on a sentient hurricane in the form of a guy.

But maybe the judges would. Once they knew the Beast was back… maybe they'd have a plan.

"Yeah."

Not taking my eyes from him, I followed the Beast away from the ocean.

# 2

## NOAH

"So…" the girl began while we started up the long wooden walkway that formed the path from the beach. "Do you have a name?"

"Noah."

My response was met with silence for a moment. "Ari."

I nodded and continued walking. It was hard, talking. Walking around. Things I'd done my whole life—the greliaran part of my whole life—suddenly felt as complicated as advanced theoretical mathematics. It'd taken me months just to get a handle on appearing like a human, instead of a human-shaped storm thing. I was getting better at it, but I still had to concentrate.

"And you used to be a greliaran?"

Her sandals clapped against the wooden slats, the noise hollow on the elevated surface. My feet made no sound at all. I probably needed to work on that. "Yeah."

"What happened? Did the dehaians, like… do this to you, or…?"

"No."

I could feel her waiting. It was like a pressure in the air.

"There was a girl. The Beast was going to kill her. I got in the way."

It killed me instead.

I left the last unspoken. It was only partly true. I'd felt death taking me. Felt my life slip away in one huge moment of pain and anguish and darkness. And then just before the last thought vanished from me, the Beast had been there, inside my head. In a heartbeat, it had known everything about me.

And it had stopped. I'd heard questions in my mind, nebulous and without words but questions nonetheless. The Beast had never killed something like me before. Something that was like it—a weapon created solely for destruction—but that had wanted so badly to live a normal life that it'd controlled what it had been made for and carved out a life like a regular person.

The Beast had never seen anything like that.

So it offered me a choice. I couldn't go back. My body… it wouldn't survive. But the Beast had been able to absorb magic, just as I had as a greliaran, and to an extent I wasn't sure the dehaians or landwalkers had even realized. It'd been able to use magic as well. It could change itself, absorb me, and together we would both have a chance at living. Or it could let me die.

There hadn't been much to decide.

"But how—" Ari started.

I glanced back at her. At about five foot six, if I had to guess, and maybe seventeen, the girl was a bizarre mix. On the one hand, she looked almost willfully ordinary. Despite the party, she hardly wore any makeup, and although her emerald dress fit her slender form well, it was incredibly plain compared to the fancier things I'd seen at that event. Her golden-brown hair was left to hang loose past her shoulders and everything about her seemed designed to convey a message that she should be overlooked.

But her eyes were a different story. Exotic, almost, and strangely captivating. Gray as rainclouds, they gave this odd impression like, to her, everything was fleeting and she already could see the decades passing by.

It was the weirdest thing.

"The Beast wanted to live," I answered. "To have a real life, beyond the half-aware existence the dehaians had given it. And I didn't want to die."

She seemed to consider that. "When was this?"

"Last summer."

Ari was quiet again. "So you—I mean, the Beast—you've been back this whole time?"

"Yeah."

"Where were you?"

Her tone was skeptical, like she couldn't figure out why no one had noticed me.

"Around."

I didn't want to get into it. I'd checked in on Baylie and Chloe a few times early on—enough to make sure they were okay, though I'd never come too close. But I'd also spent months drifting through the ocean as barely more than the amorphous, invisible consciousness that was the Beast in its resting state. Anything else was too difficult. After the output of destroying the Sylphaen, after the output of taking magic from Chloe to change the dehaians and landwalkers back to the way they'd once been, I had nothing left. The power that I—the Beast, whatever—drew from the dehaians going back and forth between the ocean and the land had taken forever to give me enough energy to do anything but exist.

And after that… it'd just been hard. Complicated.

Painful.

"Around," she repeated.

I didn't respond. Whether or not I was helping this girl didn't mean I owed her an explanation about my life. I was only talking this much because it'd been nearly a year since my last conversation with another person and I figured I needed the practice.

But it was getting awkward. More so, anyway. And she didn't need to know everything about me. It was probably better if she didn't, in fact. She was a wizard, a member of a race that I'd been fairly certain had been wiped out centuries ago. Even finding out about Joseph last year had been a shock, but I'd assumed he was just an anomaly.

To discover that dozens, maybe *hundreds,* of them were still alive…

It was disturbing and not just because, depending on the part of me, they'd either created my kind or I'd been created to destroy them. From the looks of it, they were powerful. That mansion and the cars I'd seen parked outside of it all looked like they belonged to multimillionaires. And meanwhile, it seemed as though they'd gone completely undetected by the landwalkers, despite all the elders' connections with the government and the police…

Disturbing wasn't the half of it. The Beast part of me was wary about it too. It didn't want to hurt Ari, though. Not yet. It wasn't even sure I *could*, at least not by draining her magic and killing her like I… we… it… had been created to do.

I grimaced, fighting the urge to rub my forehead, if only because it'd probably freak the wizard girl out. I hated it when my thoughts blurred like that. When I couldn't figure out how to think about myself, whether I was a greliaran with the Beast in his mind or the Beast with a greliaran skin or neither one at all—

"You okay?" Ari asked cautiously.

I bit back a curse. She'd noticed. "Yeah."

We kept walking. I could feel her watching me. I wondered how long it'd be till she tried something with that bizarre magic of hers. I'd seen her stumble after taking down that group of dehaians on the beach. She'd seemed to be struggling to stand for quite some time afterward, though that didn't necessarily mean much. That she was scared of me was fairly obvious. She'd tried to bolt two seconds after I told her what I was. But now she might just be biding her time.

I didn't know if she could actually hurt me, though. I somehow doubted it. But whatever she had was a magic that I—the *Beast*—hadn't felt before. It was alien to me, and hadn't registered on my radar as existing at all.

And meanwhile, contact with me seemed to damn near

torture her.

I winced. I hadn't meant for that to happen. I'd tried to be so careful when I lifted her up not to drain any magic from her. With my abilities, even *touching* someone with magic in them might unintentionally set me to taking it from them if I wasn't careful. I didn't want to accidentally kill the person I was attempting to help. And that scream she'd given, the *pain* in it…

It'd been horrible. I'd returned her to land as fast as I could.

I didn't want to risk hurting her like that again.

We reached the end of the long walkway from the beach. The pale sand and grass turned into a large parking lot ahead, which was empty at this hour. Beyond that lay an equally empty road with further sand and grass on its opposite side. The land to my left was as featureless as that to my right, and nothing around us gave the slightest indication of where to find more civilization. As it was, I'd only guessed at what state we were in based on the general curve of the coastline, and how it reminded me of a map I'd drawn in elementary school.

Which sucked, as directions went.

I hesitated. I did have one option, but it might make her panic. She could attack me and I *really* didn't want some instinctive reaction making me kill her in defense.

We could also be wandering out here for hours.

I glanced to Ari. Her brow drew down warily at something in my expression.

"I'm going to find out where we should go," I said. "Just… give me a second. And don't freak out."

The look on her face didn't change. I tried to ignore it while I retreated a few yards farther away.

Just in case.

She didn't take her eyes off of me.

I let my human form go.

My awareness exploded outward, going instantly from vaguely localized senses of sight and smell and hearing to all of them at once, coming from everywhere. I rushed upward and away from the parking lot as fast as I could, hoping not to hurt her. When I reached several hundred feet up, I slowed, everything that was me spread invisibly over the parking lot and beyond.

And it felt incredible, the easing of that pressure that had held me in human form. The awareness of everything around me and the way I could experience all of it at once. The flying.

God, I *loved* flying.

I made myself focus on the world below me. There was a neighborhood down the road from the beach, about two miles to the north beyond the next rise. A gas station lay beyond it, the parking lot lights blinding in the darkness. The south held nothing. A nature preserve, maybe. Humans wouldn't leave a stretch of beach that empty without a reason.

And Ari wasn't running. I noticed that too. Scanning the sky above her, she seemed shocked, but she wasn't bolting like before.

Maybe she just didn't know where to go.

I pushed the thought away, annoyed. I needed to concentrate.

The world pulled back in. The flood of sensation narrowed,

condensed, and arranged itself again. I focused on skin, on clothes, on what I'd looked like before I'd sort of quasi-died.

I opened my eyes. I checked myself over with a glance. I really was getting better at this. No problems with storm-spots on my skin or missing clothes this time.

Ari was staring at me when I turned to her.

"There's a gas station that way." I twitched my head toward the north.

She didn't respond. With my residual awareness of the air around me, I realized I couldn't even pick up on her breathing.

I started walking, figuring I may as well get distance if she ended up trying to attack.

It was a moment before I heard her follow.

"So, um, how far to the station?" Ari asked.

"A few miles."

She was silent. Gravel crunched under my shoes. In spite of everything, my lip twitched at the sound. A little more practice and I might really pass for a human again.

"And then what? You go to see these dehaians?"

I hesitated. I had to. I knew that. If Zeke had become the King of Yvaria only to turn around and send his guards to attack a bunch of people having a party on the beach…

Fury rose. I'd seen *kids* there.

"Noah?"

I struggled to push the anger aside. "Yeah, I'll go see them."

Even if I didn't want to.

"How do you know them?" Ari asked after a moment. "Did they, like, make the Beast come back? Before what happened to the greliaran part of you, I mean. Are they why you—it—returned?"

I fought back a grimace. More than anything else, *this* was what I didn't want to talk about. Chloe. The way she'd woken the Beast just by existing. Everything that'd led up to my new life.

The fact the first girl I'd ever loved was lost to me.

My grimace tried to emerge again. I'd let that go, though. I'd had to. It would have driven me mad otherwise. I couldn't have been with Chloe. Not back then and not anymore. And while yes, I'd cared for her so much, I'd thought for a while that the pain of losing any chance with her would eat me alive… the ache had faded. Slowly, but it had.

But it was still hard to face reminders of just *how much* I'd had to give up last year. It wasn't just her, or being something even *approaching* human.

There was so much more to living as the Beast than that.

I sighed. I still had to go. Whether or not Chloe was there, I needed to know what the Yvarians were doing. If there was a reason for it. Something I wasn't seeing.

I realized Ari was waiting for a response.

"They're friends. That's all."

She seemed to hear the tension in my voice. We kept going in silence.

The rise of the road fell behind us and houses appeared up ahead. Three stories tall or more, the homes glared out at the coast as though they fully intended to remain standing even if the ocean came sweeping in. None of the residents seemed to be up at this hour, however. Nearly every window was dark and only a few porch lights shone, their glow falling far short of us.

Another curve of the road passed. The gas station came into view. An old payphone clung to the building's wall.

Ari made a small noise, sounding relieved. Her footsteps quickened. We crossed the cracked concrete of the parking lot and I noticed that, just like me, she automatically steered clear of the view of the attendant inside the station.

Graffiti chiseled with ballpoint pen covered the phone booth that hung from the grimy siding. Biting her lip, Ari lifted the receiver and hit zero to place a collect call.

I turned away, watching the station and the neighborhood around it. A few security cameras were perched on the roof near us, one of them facing our way. I grimaced. I'd have to make sure I was *far* out of sight of those—and any others in the area, for that matter—before I left.

"Maia?"

Ari's voice was filled with worry. I glanced back to her.

"Are you alright?"

I waited. It was weird. Since becoming the Beast, I'd lost the ability to hear like a greliaran. Time was, I could've picked up on every word coming from the other end of the phone and, on a quiet night like this, probably the footsteps of someone a quarter mile away as well. Other things had disappeared too: my ability to detect the presence of other greliarans, the boiling hot power that used to change my skin and eyes into greliaran form. The Beast side of me felt different too; smaller over- all, perhaps, than the massive size it'd had a year before. Not empathic in the way it'd once been either—at least not with just *anyone*. I was still learning the cost of what had happened to create this new existence of mine, but it felt almost as if both sides of me had made a compromise, each sacrificing some aspects of their original nature so the whole could survive.

But it made me wonder what else had changed.

"Dhanya's okay, though?"

My attention returned to her while Ari nodded at whatever she heard on the other end of the call, the relief on her face clear. "And my mom?" A moment passed. "Good."

Her voice was tight and carefully controlled. She cast a quick look toward me before she spoke again. "Listen, Maia. I, um… I need someone to come pick me up. It's a long story, but I'm… I'm in Massachusetts."

She winced. I could almost imagine the reaction she was getting, even if I didn't know these people at all.

I looked away again. When it came to remaining unnoticed, I hadn't done the best job tonight. But I couldn't have just let the dehaians murder people in front of me.

At my back, I could hear her giving an address and I glanced over curiously before noticing the sticker on the payphone that marked the device as property of the station. The city and street address of the place were there as well.

"Thank you," Ari said. "Love you, Maia. Hug Dhanya for me."

She hung up.

"They alright?" I asked.

She blinked and looked to me. "Yeah."

I nodded. I wasn't sure why I cared; I didn't know these people and they were wizards besides. I'd tried to stop the dehaians, though. I'd gone invisible briefly and struck them as wind to slow them down, but they'd already taken out a few before I reached them.

Maybe I was just glad more people hadn't died.

"So they're coming?"

"Yeah," she said again.

I checked around. That was good. It'd still take them some time, though, assuming these ruanir people didn't ride brooms or whatever. And while yes, I needed to go find out about the Yvarians, I also didn't want to leave some girl in a bedraggled evening gown standing all by herself at a gas station in the middle of the night.

She was a wizard. She could probably take care of herself.

It was still a crappy thing to do.

"So…" Ari began.

I looked back at her.

"I guess that's it then," she said. "You… you know. Do that—" She twitched her chin. "—and go."

I paused, my nascent impulse toward chivalry or just being a good person dying at something in her voice. Fear, maybe. Or revulsion. Like she wanted me as far from her as possible, and now. "Yeah."

My voice was cold. I couldn't help it. She only nodded, though.

With a glance to the empty parking lot, I started away from her.

"Thank you," she called.

I stopped. In that thin, ripped emerald dress, she stood beside the payphone, watching me.

"You're welcome."

I continued into the neighborhood. The houses were annoyingly far apart and there weren't many trees or bushes behind which to hide. Weaving through the spaces between them, I scanned the darkened windows, hoping no one glanced out and called whatever passed for the police in this town with reports of someone sneaking around.

A cluster of bushes finally came into view. I slipped behind them quickly.

My awareness spread as my human form vanished. Rising up into the sky, I scanned the area around me and then paused when I spotted Ari sitting on the curb near the gas station payphone. Her knees were drawn close to her chest and she rubbed her arms like she was freezing. Her gaze swept the dark neighborhood and the gas station as if trying to watch every direction at once.

The dehaians could come here too. Or some utterly human predator could take advantage of a girl by herself.

I had no idea how these ruanir and their magic worked.

Frustration moved through me. I stayed put, invisible in the hazy clouds, watching her in case anything went wrong before her friends arrived.

## 3

# ARI

The breeze cut through my dress like the fabric wasn't even there. I pulled my knees tighter against my chest and chafed my arms, trying to stay warm.

I wondered if he had left yet.

I wondered if he was up there, watching me.

My shivering strengthened. That'd been… I didn't know what that'd been. Back at the parking lot, he'd been standing in front of me one minute and the next, he'd seemed to turn to mist and vanish completely.

Not mist. Clouds, all containing so much energy they'd hurt. He'd started upward and then disappeared, like he'd evaporated into nothing in only the blink of an eye, taking the pain with him.

It'd been terrifying.

Sort of.

My hold tightened on my arms. Whatever. He was gone. Probably, anyway.

I resisted the urge to look up at the sky.

Minutes slid by, creeping hopefully toward the hour or more that it'd take Maia to get someone here. I couldn't go inside to check—my appearance would raise *way* too many questions— but I wished I'd worn a watch.

The breeze died down. Night birds called in the darkness. I wondered how late it actually was.

A black limousine pulled down the street, heading my way. I pushed to my feet, eyeing it. Maia had sent a limo? That wasn't her style.

But then, Maia had mentioned Mom was with her when I asked if they were all okay.

My stomach sank.

The vehicle turned into the parking lot. Curving past the potholes in the concrete, it avoided the pump shelter com- pletely and came to a stop only a few yards from me. Mom's driver—one of them, anyway—climbed out. Despite whatever hour it was, his suit was immaculate and his black hat was too. He hurried around to open the back door on my side of the vehicle.

"My apologies for the delay, Miss Moreau."

"No problem," I replied, attempting to sound calm and probably failing.

Cautiously, I walked to the car door. Bending down, I checked to see if Mom was in there.

Nothing. The limo was empty, except for a garment bag on the seat.

Breathing a little easier, I climbed in. While the man shut the door behind me with a dull thud, I shifted around uncomfortably, the black leather of the seat making bunches of the fabric of my torn dress.

The driver returned to the wheel. "Madam Corvienne sent clothing," he explained with a nod to the bag. "I'll close the divider while you change. She has asked, however, that I bring you to the hotel as quickly as possible, so with your permission, I'll start back immediately."

I nodded my agreement and then unzipped the bag while he rolled up the visor between the driver's area and the rest of the limo. Gravity rocked me slightly when he accelerated.

Another evening gown met my gaze, this one ten times as decorative as the one I'd worn to the party. Silver and sparkly, it felt like chain mail made of sequins in my hand and it glinted like a thousand tiny mirrors in the meager light that passed through the smoked windows.

I grimaced. Of course she wouldn't just send jeans and a t-shirt. Not my mother. But given the hour this was a bit excessive, even for her.

I pressed the intercom button. "Hey."

"Yes, Miss Moreau?" the driver answered.

"My mom sent a dress. A fancy one. Is there something going on that I should know about?"

"I'm not certain, Miss. She didn't tell me anything except to pick you up and bring you to the hotel."

My mouth tightened while I regarded the dress. She was up to something and I could only hope it didn't involve Logan. I may not have any magic left in me right now, but that wouldn't stop me from giving that guy a black eye if he came near me again.

"Okay," I said to the driver. "Thanks."

I let the intercom button go. With a sigh, I tugged the dress the rest of the way from the bag and then set it aside. The emerald dress peeled like a second skin from me, and I grimaced at the clammy feeling of dirt and moisture that still clung to me. Shifting around awkwardly on the seat, I managed to pull the ridiculous silver dress over my hips and chest, and then fastened the solitary tie it possessed around my neck. My back was completely bare and the sequined fabric gaped in two long gashes that exposed most of my legs. The rest of me glittered, however.

I wondered if I could get satellite signals with this thing.

Chuckling quietly, I stuffed my ruined dress back into the bag and then turned to the window. The tiny town was already behind us, and the limo was racing down the country road toward whatever interstate led out of this place.

I didn't mind. Dress aside, I couldn't wait to get back. Maia and Dhanya were okay, although Dhanya had barely escaped. If it hadn't been for all of our magic stirring up a wind that slowed the dehaians, they would have killed her.

I swallowed hard. They were fine, though. Mom was too. I'd be back at the hotel soon and this crazy night would finally be over.

The limo continued on, joining the interstate traffic toward Maine and then leaving it once we finally reached Portland. The driver wove his way toward the hotel, pulling up at last by the glass double doors of the massive brick building. Golden light shone through the windows, though at this hour, curtains obscured the interior. The street around us was so empty, it left me feeling like I was in a post-apocalyptic movie.

Nearly empty, anyway.

Two figures shrugged away from the walls inside the hotel entryway. Despite the suits they wore, the men appeared unremarkable with their nondescript brown hair and medium builds.

But that didn't stop me from tensing. There was something that gave them away—to my kind, in any case. Enforcers. They had to be. I didn't even need to see their eyes change to be sure. That casual, predatory grace in the way they moved; that calm gaze like they could kill anything that got in their way… they may as well have worn signs. And where they were, a judge couldn't be far behind. This wasn't like at the mansion. There, I'd expected to see judges.

This was something else entirely.

I'd vanished from the party. I'd ended up a hundred miles away.

I should have known that would draw the Judiciary's attention.

The driver opened the door and I could sense his nervousness in the tight way he moved. He was human and he didn't know what we were, but even without that, he'd still spent enough time around us to recognize those guys as dangerous. His face was like cardboard when he held the door for me. He never looked at the two men once.

I climbed from the limo, fighting hard to keep from

appearing anxious myself. The enforcers wouldn't hurt me. That couldn't be why they were here. I hadn't done any magic that humans would have seen, I wouldn't *dare* touch ocean magic, and as for how I ended up in Massachusetts… the Beast wasn't my fault. I could just tell the judge what had happened and the Judiciary would understand. They'd be sympathetic—or as close to it as their dispassionate, impartial selves were capable of. It'd be fine.

Why'd they bring *enforcers*, though?

Drawing a breath, I forced myself to stand up straighter as I walked toward the door. The enforcers made no move to open it, watching me instead while I pulled the brass handle of the glass door and then continued toward them.

"Can I help you?" I asked.

A smirk twitched the lip of the one on my left. He jerked his head toward the elevator. "Upstairs."

"The suite?"

His expression said I was stupid for having asked. I kept going and attempted to appear calm when they turned in unison to follow me.

It wasn't easy.

The glistening door of the elevator pulled back, revealing the wood-paneled interior. I walked inside. The two enforcers came after me in utter silence.

Not looking at them, I pressed the button for the correct floor.

Seconds crawled past. The arrow on the old-fashioned dial above the elevator door ticked across the numbers with all the speed of a dying snail.

The door opened onto a hallway of cream carpet and golden light fixtures, with bars of dark wood trim in between. On shaking legs, I left the elevator and walked toward our suite. I couldn't hear the enforcers follow.

That didn't mean anything.

Swallowing hard, I knocked on the door. The sound seemed like a dull thud in the silence. My palms were sweating and I resisted the urge to swipe them on the absurd silver dress while I waited for someone to respond.

But I wished this damn dress had a back on it. *Anything* between me and the enforcers would have been nice.

Mom opened the door. "Ariabella! You're back!"

She said it like my presence was a pleasant surprise. And like there weren't two enforcers standing a yard away.

Stepping aside, she pulled the door open wider.

I walked into the suite. Everything was neutral tones of eggshell and brown, from the leather couch and chairs to the indifferently patterned carpet. The curtains on the floor-to-ceiling windows overlooking the city were closed and the lamps on the end tables cast gray shadows and buttercream light on the room. Judge Engle sat on the couch, one leg crossed atop the other and a full cup of coffee untouched on the table beside him. Another enforcer waited nearby, this one blond with a build and a stance like he was the poster child for the Marines. At the table on the far left side of the room, a trio of slender, dark-haired women in black evening gowns watched me and the judge equally.

My stomach clenched. The judge's assistants. The people who served like living versions of the jewelry I wore to store magical energy, just in case I needed it.

But I'd be fine, I reminded myself. The assistants travelled everywhere with the judges and really, the enforcers often did too. This didn't mean the Judiciary was upset with me. They didn't have any reason to be. I hadn't endangered the ruanir.

Except for telling the Beast we still existed, anyway.

I clenched my teeth, fighting to keep my jaw from trembling. They'd understand that too. The judges were impartial for a reason and that reason was our protection. No nepotism, no bias. They protected us from ocean magic at tremendous cost to themselves and they evaluated everything with utter fairness.

They'd understand the situation I'd been placed in.

Jace rose from a chair, his gray eyes locked on me. Beneath the flop of his light mahogany hair, stress showed on his face, owing maybe as much to his worry for me as it did to the adjustment.

"Are you alright?" he asked me.

"Jace," Mom hissed. "Manners."

His jaw tightened.

Judge Engle ignored them both. Pushing away from the couch, he stood. His black suit hung from him in precise lines that gave no indication of the late hour and his dark hair was combed back from his tall forehead. He wasn't as old as many of the other judges—his hair was only starting to go gray around the temples—and his face had that sharp-edged look that meant he'd probably been a heartthrob when he was younger. He'd also been a friend of my grandmother's and the only one of the judges that I could ever remember smiling at me when I was a child.

He didn't look so friendly now.

"Ariabella Moreau," he said, his voice like a black pond on a windless day.

"Yes, sir?"

"You are to be examined in connection with tonight's events. Do you object?"

I saw Jace tense. I couldn't even breathe. Wait, examined? "W-why do you need to—"

"Do you object?"

I floundered, my shock drying up into fear. There wasn't any other response to give. Not with enforcers behind me. Not with a judge asking the question. "No, sir."

The three women rose from the table. One of them lifted a chair and brought it with her as they came toward us. She set it in front of Judge Engle.

He motioned to the chair. "Have a seat."

I walked over and sat down. Two of the women stayed beside me, while the third went to stand next to the judge.

She laid her hand in his. I shivered, not taking my eyes from them. He lifted his arm, his palm facing upward, and a smooth river stone was cupped within it.

The air cooled on my skin, like I'd just walked into a cave where the atmosphere was heavy from moisture and centuries without the sun. The feeling spread over my body, chilling the anxious sweat on my back and cloying onto my skin like plastic wrap.

And then the coldness sank into me. My teeth clenched while I fought to keep from panicking. The sensation went deeper, freezing past my muscles and bones to reach into my very organs, and then crawling through them, examining everything that was me.

It felt like death. I closed my eyes; tears leaked past my lids. I couldn't breathe. I didn't *want* to breathe. The warmth of the world would hurt against the moist decay filling my lungs.

And then the sensation pulled back and vanished. I gasped, my eyes opening.

Judge Engle still stood in front of me. The assistant dropped her hand from his and stumbled aside. Breathing hard, she caught herself on the couch and nearly fell onto it. The other two women paused, waiting for a sign Judge Engle required them. When none came, they hurried over to help their companion.

The judge paid them no attention. His gaze dropped to regard the stone in his hand, now catching the light with a sickly green tone. Folding his fingers over it, he turned away from me.

My brother appeared at my side and threw a blanket around my shoulders. Pulling me up from the chair, he wrapped me in his arms and held me against him.

I clung to him, unable to stop shivering. Jace's support felt like the only thing that kept me standing.

"Release her," Judge Engle ordered.

Jace froze. "What?"

"She has been exposed to ocean magic."

I felt Jace's breath catch. "Is she alright? Did she take any of it in?"

"*Release* her, Mister Moreau."

Jace stared at him for a heartbeat and then carefully helped me back into the chair.

"Did I?" My teeth chattered as much from fear as the residual effects of the judge's magic. "Take it in, I mean?"

"What happened this evening?" the judge asked rather than respond. He pinned me with the calm, penetrating gaze that characterized his kind.

And suddenly I couldn't find words.

"You vanished during the assault on my home," he stated. "Less than an hour later, you contacted your cousin, Miss Davenport, from a gas station in Massachusetts. What passed in the interim?"

I shivered. "There was a... a guy. On the beach."

Mom made an infuriated sound, though stress turned it nearly into a squeak. "A boy? You ran off with a *boy* while people were *dying*? How could you—"

"Madam Corvienne," the judge interrupted.

She blanched. Judge Engle's gaze returned to me.

"He wasn't a boy." I drew a steadying breath. "He told me he was the Beast."

On the couch, the assistants looked up, the first expression I'd seen from them on their faces.

Alarm. And they weren't alone. From the corner of my eye,

I could see Mom staring at me, while Jace just seemed to have frozen.

Judge Engle's expression didn't change.

"He was lying," Mom snapped.

I didn't look away from the judge. He hadn't stopped watching me. I couldn't read anything of what he thought from his face.

"It took you away from the dehaians," Judge Engle stated.

The words were like a question and a confirmation of what he already knew at the same time.

I nodded. "They were chasing me. He picked me up. Carried me away from them."

Mom gave an incredulous scoff. "It can't have been the *Beast*. That's not—"

"It spoke with you," the judge said.

Mom's mouth clamped shut.

I nodded again. "A-a bit." At his silence, I continued. "He, um… *it* wanted to know how the ruanir were still alive. It claimed not to be under the control of dehaians anymore. That it knew them, but didn't work for them." I paused. "It was pretty emphatic about that part."

The judge's lips thinned. "Very well."

He motioned to one of the men behind me and then started for the door. His assistants moved to follow.

"Wait," Mom protested. "That's all? Judge Engle, shouldn't you take her with you? If she's contagious—"

He turned back to her. "Your daughter will be watched. She has been exposed to ocean magic, yes, and she may require additional examination. Thus Hans will remain. If she shows any sign of ill effects from the exposure, he will contact us immediately." He nodded briefly to the blond enforcer before returning his gaze to Mom. "The rest is a matter for the Judiciary."

My stomach twisted at the words. I didn't want to go through any examinations again.

Or to think that there was even a *chance* I had ocean magic inside my system.

"But…" Mom floundered. She seemed to be waging a war against her desire to argue and the identity of the person to whom she was protesting. "But it *can't* have been the *Beast*, though. It's a myth. A metaphor. She can't have *met* the thing. It doesn't *exist!*"

Judge Engle didn't answer. His assistants trailed him into the hall. One of the enforcers followed them and shut the door at their back.

The other didn't move. Only a few yards from me, Hans folded his hands and stood like he intended to remain there for eternity.

But his pale gaze didn't leave me. A smirk twitched his lip when he saw me watching him, and for a heartbeat, his eyes flashed into solid yellow-green orbs like a snake's, slit by black.

I flinched. I couldn't help it.

The smirk grew. His eyes returned to their normal blue shade.

Mom didn't notice. "Ariabella," she snapped. "Stop this nonsense."

I didn't respond.

Mom made an incredulous noise. Shaking her head, she walked away.

"Come on," Jace said, nodding toward the room we shared. He eyed the enforcer. "We'll just be in here."

I could hear his hope that the man wouldn't follow in his voice.

Hans was motionless.

I retreated with Jace into the next room. He shut the door behind us.

"Are you okay?" he asked. "Really?"

I wasn't sure what to say. I crossed to my bed, the leftmost of the two in the room and the nearest to the broad window. Sinking down onto the edge of the mattress, I looked to the view beyond the sheer hotel curtains.

Jace sat down next to me with a small sigh.

"A-are you?" I asked him, glancing to him worriedly.

He nodded. "I'm fine. Worst is probably over, according to the doctors." He paused. "What happened, Ari?"

I returned my gaze to the view of the city. "I don't know. You heard about the attack?"

"Dehaians," he confirmed. "Though how that's even *possible*..."

"We weren't that far from the ocean."

"But why would they just attack us? Assuming they even *knew* who they were attacking."

"They didn't seem shocked by us fighting back."

He paused. "Did you have to?"

I fidgeted with the edge of the white bedspread. He seemed

to catch sight of my destroyed ring for the first time.

"Ari?" he asked, his voice hardening.

"Took everything I had."

Quickly, his hand came to rest on mine. The amber beads of the prayer bracelet he wore flared like candles lit them from within.

I pulled away sharply. "What are you doing?" Alarmed, I stared at him. "Jace, if there's even a *trace* of this in me—"

"It's not. You heard the judge. Exposed, not absorbed. You think they'd have you sitting here if there was a chance of an outbreak?"

I didn't know how to respond. Judge Engle hadn't said that, not exactly, and regardless, Jace still shouldn't risk sharing magic with me. The energy in the ocean was toxic beyond words; even exposure was dangerous. But he also loved me. We'd been all each other had for years, since Dad had always been busy and Mom was never a part of our lives till recently.

Protective was his default.

"And this Beast thing?" he asked.

I shook my head helplessly.

"It didn't hurt you?"

I hesitated. "I'm okay. There was some pain when he picked me up, but—"

"It picked you *up*?"

"To save my life."

Jace was silent.

"The dehaians were going to kill me. He grabbed me and—" I chuckled desperately. "—and that's how I ended up in Massachusetts. It hurt, Jace. But I don't think he meant it to."

I looked away again. Now that I was back here, safe in the hotel with Jace, the night started to feel different. Noah could have killed me. He was the Beast. He'd been designed to destroy us. That was his entire purpose.

And instead he'd protected me. Taken me to safety. Stayed with me to make sure I found a phone. He had more magic at his disposal than anyone I'd ever seen...

He'd almost seemed afraid of hurting someone with it.

"Maybe," Jace allowed, his tone leaving little room for the possibility. "But if this thing is real... Ari, it's a monster. A soulless, merciless monster. You know the stories."

I grimaced. I couldn't reconcile it—the guy who said he'd joined up with the Beast and now things were different, versus the creature that I'd grown up terrified would wake from its sleep and destroy us all.

"He told me—"

"And the dehaians probably ordered it to lie."

"Why?"

"Any number of reasons!" Jace stared at me like he couldn't understand why I didn't see his point.

I turned away.

Jace let out a breath, rising from the bedside. "Look, I don't know, alright? It just doesn't seem likely that a centuries-old killing machine could miraculously change like that. And then for it to show up *right* as dehaians attack us for the first time in centuries?" He made a disbelieving noise. "Don't you think it's all a bit convenient?"

I didn't respond.

"Ari."

"What?" I snapped, looking up at him.

He paused. "I just want you to stay safe, alright? Safe from this thing and safe from—" His gaze darted to the door. "All the rest of it."

I let out a breath, closing my eyes. He sank back onto the bed.

"I'm sorry," he sighed. "I don't mean to be a jerk. I just—"

"You're not." I grimaced. "And I'm sorry too."

He nodded.

"It doesn't matter now anyway," I said.

"It hurt you."

"But he's gone. It's over."

Jace's gaze returned to the door. "Yeah."

He didn't sound like he believed the response.

I followed his gaze. I knew what the enforcer's presence meant. The Judiciary was still watching me. Us. It was impossible to tell what they thought about all this.

But I knew I was right. Noah was gone and we would be heading back to Chicago soon. Whatever was going on with the dehaians and the Beast, our little piece of it had to be done.

# 4

## NOAH

In the air outside the hotel, I watched the girl walk into the building like she was going to the gallows. I couldn't tell what had upset her. She'd been tense since the limo showed up, which had bothered me. She'd almost backed away from it at the gas station and when she'd approached the car door, she'd looked like she was waiting for something to attack her.

Pretty much the same as she'd looked walking into the hotel.

Annoyance moved through me. It wasn't my problem. It *really* wasn't. So the girl was tense. I'd done my part, getting her away from the dehaians. If her own people freaked her out, that was her business.

I wished I knew why they upset her, though.

Wind swept around me while I moved away from the hotel. It probably had nothing to do with tonight's events and everything to do with her own life and things I'd never know about. But meanwhile, there was a fine line between making sure someone was safe and stalking, and I was probably approaching the latter.

Even if I *was* curious about these ruanir. About what their existence could mean for me—all of me. Both sides of me were in complete agreement for once and wanted to know more.

And wanted to put off seeing the dehaians as long as possible.

My annoyance grew. I was leery of dehaians, owing mostly to the Beast part of me, though the greliaran had his fair share of reservations too. The Beast had been tortured by them. Its whole creation stemmed from ocean magic forcibly condensed down and bound to the dehaians' will. It'd broken free and damn near destroyed their world as payback, and although now it was willing to accept the idea that maybe not *all* of them were terrible, the wariness remained.

And the greliaran side of me would rather just forget about this and return to the other end of the planet where I'd spent a good chunk of the last year.

But if Zeke was starting a war…

I moved faster. It'd take me a while to reach him. Traveling between the oceans was difficult, considering that my only options consisted of circling the land or going across it. The first took more time, and the second meant going where the currents of magic drifting up from the sea were weaker. I'd opted for a compromise of the two, circling toward Mexico and over it, if only because crossing the United States would slow me down.

For so many reasons.

I pushed the thought aside. I'd talk to Baylie eventually. Mom, Dad, and everyone else too.

Hours passed. So did the night. The morning sun chased

me when I reached the Pacific.

I headed down.

Water engulfed me. It felt hardly any different than the air. I'd figured out fairly quickly that breathing wasn't really an issue for me. In my human form, I kept it going for the sake of seeming like everyone else—though I had to remind myself about it most of the time—and when I was like this, it didn't seem to matter at all.

The seafloor rushed by, dotted with hills and valleys and jumbled rocks. The wreckage of an old ship slipped past, its shape mostly lost to rust and decay, as did random garbage fallen from the world above. The water grew darker from the increasing depth, though it did little to stop me from picking up on the terrain all around with some weird form of extrasensory perception.

Though that wasn't the only thing.

Chloe's presence appeared on the horizon, tugging at my mind. She wasn't bothering to hide that signal coming off of her anymore—the signal that had woken the Beast from its centuries of sleep and sent that part of me after her a year ago. But like so much else, even that had changed with my new life. Despite how Chloe and her magic had helped me alter the dehaians and landwalkers last year, they didn't show up to me like she did. Beyond their physical forms, they didn't show up at all. The signal seemed tied to the quasi-empathic connection I still had with her and Baylie.

It made her like a blazing supernova in a pitch-black night.

I headed toward her. Minutes raced past. The veil around

Nyciena fell behind me and in the blink of an eye, lights and dehaians and homes inside rock spires all came into view.

They hadn't changed the veil to try to defend against me, I noticed. Considering how the Beast had torn through the city a year before, I appreciated the gesture of trust now.

I continued toward the mountain at the heart of Nyciena and the palace that the Beast side of me remembered that it housed. The city had mostly been repaired since the Beast's attack last summer, though pockets of damage still remained. The dehaians around me didn't seem to notice my presence, though. Even with their ability to detect shapes around them in the water, none of them were reacting at all. But then, in this state, I was only energy not form; there probably wasn't anything for them to pick up on.

The secondary veil around the mountain fell behind me. Chloe was somewhere on a middle level of the palace. I wondered if she knew I was around yet.

I wondered what would happen if I took human form here, now, with no warning. I hadn't tried it yet near dehaians. They might panic.

Maybe I should have waited outside the city.

Consternation moved through me while I eyed the guards hovering beside the cave openings that served as windows and doors on the palace. They could panic regardless of where I showed up. And it wasn't like I wanted to spend the next few hours waiting for them to decide to let me back into the city, or give them the opportunity to evacuate the king before I even had a chance to talk to him.

The Beast part of me argued that if they *were* starting a war, maybe scaring them wouldn't be such a bad idea. The last thing I wanted was people fighting with magic. That's what had ended me up in this situation.

Oh, hell with it.

My awareness condensed. Dehaian guards shouted in alarm.

Floating in the water, I flicked my gaze down quickly, making sure I looked human, and then returned my attention to the dehaians. Spikes on their arms, they sped toward me, though a few broke off to race back inside and raise further alerts.

I didn't move.

Another group of guards came from the palace and I recognized the one in the center. Bronze-scaled and dark-haired, with a patch over one eye and a scar extending across his face on either side of it. Tiberion, the leader of Zeke's soldiers.

He didn't look happy.

"Why have you come here?" he demanded the moment he came close.

"I want to speak with Zeke."

Tiberion's face darkened. "The King of Yvaria cannot simply be summoned—"

"I'm not. I'm asking. But this is important. I need to talk to him."

The man was silent. He had about a million reasons for hating me, I knew. After all, he'd still have both eyes if not for what the Beast had done.

But Zeke hadn't changed the defenses on the city. And while I wasn't sure the dehaians *could* keep me out, they hadn't even *tried.*

I had to hope that counted for something.

"I don't mean anyone here harm," I added.

Tiberion's mouth tightened. His eyes ran over me quickly. "Send word to his majesty," he snapped over his shoulder at one of the others.

The woman nodded and took off toward the castle. Another guard emerged from the palace before she'd even made it halfway there.

I couldn't hear their conversation, but the woman sped back as quickly as she'd left.

"The king will see him," she murmured to Tiberion.

Tiberion scowled. He jerked his head toward the palace, not taking his eyes from me. "This way."

He motioned for the guards to surround me. Reluctance flashed across a few of their faces, but they obeyed.

We headed for the highest level of the palace and in no time we'd passed the tall stand of bright green leaves that the dehaians used for doors. The dark stone of the hall surrounded us, the surface inlaid with gold and gemstones that picked out patterns of various territories, all of which I suspected were within the Kingdom of Yvaria. The map glittered in the blue-white flames that burned in the lamps overhead, the whole thing like a massive reminder of wealth and power, writ large across the walls.

I wondered if Zeke had done this. I really didn't know him that well, but it didn't strike me as his style.

Maybe it'd been one of the previous rulers.

The guards turned at a door halfway down the hall. Tiberion entered ahead of me, while another soldier held back the leaves in the doorway. I followed the commander inside.

Zeke was waiting. He didn't look any different from a year ago, but then dehaians aged slower than humans anyway. There wasn't much reason he would have changed.

Except for being king, anyway. That, I could see. He'd always had that attitude like he knew right where he fit in the world so it better damn well listen to him, but he seemed more reserved now. More cautious.

Though maybe that was because of me.

"Noah." His expression and voice gave nothing away. "Welcome."

"Thanks for seeing me."

"Why are you here?"

I tried not to grimace. Right to the point. Well, it saved me the trouble of figuring out how to ask.

"Yvarians. Last night, out by Maine, they attacked a group of people on the beach. I want to know why."

An actual expression flashed over Zeke's face this time, and it looked like alarm. "Yvarians?"

"They had the armbands of your soldiers. They ambushed those people. Killed some of them."

Zeke looked to Tiberion. "Find out about this." The commander motioned sharply to two guards, who immediately swam from the room. Zeke turned his attention back to me. "I promise you, I didn't—"

Leaves rustled behind me. "Noah?"

I tensed and looked back. Chloe hovered by the doorway, her cream scales glinting in the light and her red hair floating in the water behind her.

"Chloe," I said.

"Y-you're back. You're…" Her green eyes darted over me, incredulous. I suddenly felt painfully aware of how I hadn't looked human the last time she'd seen me. "Are you okay? I mean—" She glanced to Zeke, clearly struggling to regroup. "What's going on? Is everything alright?"

"It's—"

"Some Yvarian soldiers attacked people on the Atlantic coast," I cut in before Zeke could finish. I wanted to see her reaction. To know if she'd been aware of this, in case he was lying about any of it.

Her face was a picture of shock. "What?"

"I don't know," Zeke assured her. "Tiberion has people looking into it."

"What happened?" she asked.

"The dehaians struck first," I said. "They tried to kill anyone they saw. Shot them down with those net gun things and then…"

I left the rest unspoken. Chloe grew even more pale.

"That's not all, though," I continued. "The people who were targeted…" My gaze flicked between them. "They're not human. They're wizards."

Zeke's brow climbed. "What?"

"I thought Joseph was the last one," Chloe said.

I shook my head. "Apparently not. When the dehaians attacked, these folks fought back. Magically. But they're not like Joseph either. They seem human and they call themselves ruanir."

"You're *sure* about this?" Zeke asked.

My eyebrow twitched up. His mouth tightened.

"Did you see where the dehaians went?" Chloe asked. "Maybe they were just pretending to be Yvarian soldiers."

Zeke looked like he'd already considered the idea. He glanced to me.

I paused. "I didn't follow them."

Frustration flashed across Zeke's face. "You thought they were Yvarian, but you didn't check where they—"

"I was getting one of the ruanir out of there," I interrupted. "The dehaians had her cut off from the rest and they were chasing her down."

"Any idea how many of these *ruanir* people are out there?" Zeke asked.

"No. But they're rich. Big mansion for the party. Limousines, fancy hotels, all that. There were at least a hundred of them at that place and they're not hiding like Joseph did."

"Fancy hotels?" Chloe asked.

I hesitated. "I made sure the girl got back safe."

The weirdest series of expressions flickered over Chloe's face, ending in something almost like a hopeful smile. I looked away, uncomfortable even if I wasn't quite sure why.

"I don't know if they'll be looking for payback," I pressed on. "Or if they know enough about dehaians to tell what country those attackers were advertising that they were from. But if this wasn't Yvaria, then someone out there is trying pretty hard to make it look like you."

"It *wasn't* us," Zeke emphasized, his tone darkening.

I nodded in acknowledgement, hoping that was true.

Zeke was silent for a moment. "We'll check into it." His gaze flicked between me and Chloe. "Will you be staying long?" he asked me.

I hesitated.

"You're welcome here," he continued.

I found myself pausing again. "Thanks."

He nodded neutrally. Again, his eyes twitched toward Chloe.

"I'll be down the hall," he said like he read something in her expression. He swam past and his hand brushed Chloe's on his way out. She gave him a small smile.

Tiberion stayed by the door. So did the other guards. Silence settled over the room, awkward and thick.

Chloe glanced to them. "Could you guys…?" She bent her head toward the door.

"Your safety, my lady," Tiberion replied, clearly not intending to go anywhere.

She winced with discomfort. Flicking her tail, she swam toward the far wall of the room.

I joined her. Biting her lip, she skipped her gaze across me as if noting how easily I moved through the water, but she didn't meet my eyes.

"My lady?" I asked quietly.

The wince returned. "Titles. Zeke just… it makes things easier."

Silence came back.

"So how are you?" I tried.

Chloe looked up, her green eyes finding mine for the first time. "How are *you?*"

I shrugged.

"When did… you know, this?" She made a tiny gesture toward me.

"Few months ago."

"And are you doing alright?"

I searched for an answer, not coming up with much. "Yeah."

Silence again. I was starting to think it was the only thing the two of us would be good at anymore.

"Have you talked to Baylie?"

I didn't respond.

"You should."

"Is she okay?"

Chloe nodded, but it looked reluctant. "I think so. She's back in Santa Lucina now. Been there about a month in an apartment your dad set up for her." Chloe hesitated. "She misses you, though. We all do."

I dropped my gaze to the table beside us and the random assortment of things there.

"Will you stay for a while?" she asked.

I glanced toward the soldiers. They hadn't taken their eyes from me. They looked ready to rush over here if Chloe made the slightest sign of alarm.

"Chloe, I—"

"It might help."

I looked back to her, my brow furrowing.

"If people see you," she explained. "It might help them not be as scared."

Her gaze darted toward the guards and back to me.

She'd seen that too. But then, I supposed she'd have to be blind to have missed it.

"You're welcome here, Noah," she insisted. "Zeke meant that. You always have been."

I didn't know how to respond. It wasn't just about not feeling welcome—though, yes, that'd been a question. She was the girl I'd fallen for, now living with her royal boyfriend in his palace. Being around them… well, *uncomfortable* didn't even come close.

Though that wasn't all of the problem.

"Please," she pressed. "Stay."

My mouth tightened. I shouldn't. I didn't want to deal with this. *Any* of this. It was part of why I'd kept away, even after I knew I could look human again. Why I'd put off seeing my family.

But the look in her eyes made me grimace. I couldn't bring myself to explain. "Alright."

She smiled. I tried to give her a smile in return.

Quickly, she swam back toward the soldiers and I heard her telling them to find me a room here. From their expressions, they hated the idea. I didn't blame them. Even if our reasons were different, I did too.

They didn't want the Beast in their proximity.

I didn't want to be reminded that everyone I cared about was going to be lost to me someday.

# 5

## ARI

"Now, you understand that *none* of the hotel staff are allowed to touch our things, correct? *Only* you?"

I sighed. Stuffing my toiletries bag into my suitcase, I attempted to ignore the sound of Mom giving the driver orders for our luggage. We needed to get out of here soon if we wanted to catch our flight. At the rate she was going, though, we'd be lucky to make it home before Thanksgiving.

Though on the bright side, at least Logan hadn't shown up yet.

Jace left the bathroom. "Not exactly New Mexico, is it?" he murmured as he passed.

I grinned. "Two weeks without showers."

"I thought you were going to go crazy."

"*Me*? You were the one who nearly staged a revolt. Remember when Dad wanted to extend the trip?"

"'Better light on the other side of the mountain'," he quoted.

"Nightmare."

"Completely."

I chuckled, zipping up my bag, but only a moment passed before my smile started to fade. Hefting the suitcase, I moved it to the floor, and caught sight of the humor disappearing from Jace's expression too.

He noticed me watching him and his lip twitched ruefully. I nodded, reading the look. I missed the countless camping adventures we'd taken for the sake of Dad's art too.

In the main room, Mom followed the driver out the front door, still giving orders. Hans the Enforcer remained stationed by the entrance like a bizarre part of the hotel décor.

Jace sighed. "You doing alright?" he asked me in a low voice.

"Yeah."

I could feel his gaze on me when I headed for the dresser to make certain we hadn't left anything behind. I wasn't lying. I did feel better. Despite what Judge Engle had done, despite the ocean magic I'd been exposed to, my energy was returning.

Maybe faster than it should have.

I tugged open the drawer. When I'd kept Logan from hurting me, it'd taken me days to be able to sense any magic inside myself at all. But when I woke up this morning, I already felt like I could use magic again if I had to. Not much, but some.

It was strange.

"Ari?"

I glanced back.

"You *sure*?"

I nodded. "Yeah. What about you?"

He shrugged dismissively. "Doesn't hurt anymore. I don't really *feel* different, but…"

"Takes years for that, right?"

"Guess so."

I smiled.

He still looked like he wasn't sure he believed me about being okay.

I returned to my bag, trying to ignore the expression. Feeling fine wasn't a problem, but I knew Jace would worry about it if I told him.

The hotel suite door opened again. "Ariabella?" Mom called. Her voice sounded cheerful and tight. My blood pressure spiked while cursing ran through my head. I thought we'd missed Logan. I turned.

It was almost worse. Two more enforcers stood in the entryway behind her. Dressed in dark suits with blond crew cuts, they looked like clones of the one waiting inside the door. They glanced to Hans, and at the unspoken signal, he moved toward me.

"Your presence is required by the Judiciary," the leftmost one intoned.

Instinctively, I backpedaled. "What's wrong?"

They didn't answer. On some level, I hadn't thought they would. Enforcers never explained. That was the judges' job. Their only purpose was to make sure the judges' orders were followed.

Hans took my arm.

"Hey!" my brother protested.

"Jace!" Mom snapped.

He pulled up short of grabbing the enforcer to stop him.

"I'll go," I said to Hans. "It's fine."

I directed the last to Jace. The enforcers might hurt him if he tried to stop them. He knew that.

Jace's jaw muscles clenched. He made no move toward me, but I could see him struggling against the impulse. "May we follow?" he growled like he was biting off the words.

"It is permitted."

I couldn't tell which of the enforcers spoke. My gaze darted between Hans and the hallway while he led me from the room. The Judiciary wanted to see me. This never happened. Not unless something was very wrong. But I felt fine. More than fine. Surely that wasn't a bad thing?

The elevator car arrived. Hans didn't let go of my arm. With Jace, Mom, and the two other enforcers behind us, we walked into it.

Floors ticked by on the dial. The car slowed.

"You will not run."

I nodded at Hans' words. I wasn't that stupid.

The door opened. Hans dropped his hand from my arm.

We left the elevator. Compared to last night, the lobby was packed. Three hotel employees stood behind the front desk, no sooner answering one phone than another began to ring. People were lined up to check out and others were finishing their breakfast in the adjacent dining room. No one gave us more than a cursory glance when we walked by.

A limousine was waiting for us, but it wasn't Mom's. Several yards away, her driver stood beside her limo, eyes wide.

"Get the rest of our bags and—" Mom looked to the

enforcers. "Will we be long?"

"As long as required." The enforcer turned to the driver. "You will return their luggage to their room and arrange with the hotel staff for them to stay. Someone will call if you are needed."

The man nodded quickly. He hurried into the hotel.

"Inside," the enforcer said to me.

I climbed into the limo. Jace and Mom joined me, though an enforcer stayed between us.

The limo pulled away from the hotel.

"So what is this about?" Jace demanded.

Mom made an anxious, shushing noise.

The enforcer beside me didn't respond.

"Ari didn't do anything," Jace persisted.

"You will be told what you need to know once we arrive," the enforcer said.

Jace scowled.

We headed south, eventually leaving Portland behind. Through the darkened windows, I saw kids in the back seats of sedans pointing when the limousine passed. The thick walls muffled the road noise, leaving us in a low, rushing kind of silence that made my ears ring.

When Portland was long gone and the highway was too, we finally reached the gates of the judge's mansion. The limo came to a halt in the large circle drive of the house. A servant in a black dress hurried over to open the door of the car.

Struggling to keep my nervousness from showing, I climbed out. There were a half dozen other limousines in the driveway.

I had little doubt what it could mean.

The Judiciary was already here.

Hans took my arm again. He strode toward the mansion, giving me no choice but to follow. In the yard around me, no sign of the dehaians' attack remained. The judges would have seen to it that any bodies were removed and their deaths explained, though. But not even a damaged flower bush or grass blade gave evidence that there'd been an ambush now.

Marble steps led up to the dark double doors, one of which was standing open. On either side of the entrance and for two stories above it, the windows reflected the blue sky and showed nothing of what was going on inside.

Cool air hit me when we passed the door. The front hall was as dark as everything else, with brown marble for the floors and golden chandeliers hanging thirty feet above my head. Gilded mirrors and oil paintings lined the walls, each of them as tall as me, while a broad stairway waited at the end.

I hadn't seen the inside of the mansion. We'd gone around back to the gazebo right when we arrived last night. But somehow it was exactly as I'd expected a judge's home to be.

Which was to say opulent. And currently terrifying, though only because of the present situation. If I'd seen it last night, I probably wouldn't have thought anything of it at all.

Hans led me past an archway and through a luxuriously decorated sitting room, complete with antique furniture and Persian rugs so thick, they felt like pillows beneath my feet. Mom made nervously appreciative noises behind me, as though by approving of the décor she could somehow make this less frightening. Jace was silent, but when I glanced back, I could see him eyeing the tall windows and archways like he was plotting the fastest way for us to escape.

I made myself keep breathing. It was fine. *We* were fine.

But what could they know about me now that they hadn't been able to figure out last night?

We continued to the rear of the house, and when we walked into the parlor, it was all I could do to keep from retreating.

Six judges stood in the room, three men and three women with their forms turned to shadow and silhouette by the glare of sunlight through the windows behind them. They didn't say a word when Hans released my arm, but simply regarded us with a silence that never seemed to want to end.

Judge Engle finally stepped forward. "Ariabella Moreau, the judges have reviewed your case."

I stared at him. "What… what case?"

"You encountered a creature known as the Beast, and through this, you were exposed to an unprecedented amount of magic from the ocean—magic which is toxic to the ruanir and of which our kind long ago forswore the use, lest we draw this creature to us. The judges accept that you did not gain the attention of this creature willingly, but rather that the creature was present before the attack yesterday evening. We have known of its return for some time, and became aware of its presence before the dehaians arrived."

"Really?"

Judge Engle's mouth tightened. I wasn't supposed to ask questions. But after a brief glance to the others, he seemed to forgive the breach of etiquette. "Yes. In its incorporeal state and above water, the Beast can be tracked as an energy signature, and over the past year, it has been growing stronger. It does vanish, however, when it disappears into the deep ocean, but also—at times—when it is over land. On certain occasions, we lose track of it entirely.

"This occurred last night. At first, we registered its presence near this property prior to the dehaian attack. During the assault, however, it vanished. We were unable to locate it again until seconds after the dehaians fled, at which point we tracked it toward the location where you were found. Again it vanished, until nearly an hour later when it reappeared."

I realized what he was saying.

Judge Engle nodded. "You see the pattern. When it takes the form of a human, it disappears. The dehaians have given their weapon a new form of camouflage."

I shook my head. "He swore he didn't work for them."

"Yet after leaving you, the creature returned almost immediately to the very nation from which the attackers came."

I blinked. "I…" I wet my dry lips. "He, uh, he said he wanted to find out if they were responsible."

"A clever ruse, but a lie. It returned to its masters to report on the success of its mission. We do not know the full scale of their plans yet, but their unprovoked attack only moments after their 'Beast' registered in our proximity… Miss Moreau, matters have changed in this past year. The dehaians, so long trapped in the ocean, have regained the ability to move inland. Their landwalker allies can now travel to the coast. They've mastered the Beast once again, and even improved its design. You can see the danger here. The threat. And now for them to attack us, to attack our *children*, and to put you in danger and then 'rescue' you through use of their Beast…"

I quivered.

"The dehaians clearly have a plan," he continued, "one that endangers us all. They appear to be working at several goals, and one of those is clearly to find out how much of them we still know. It is for this purpose the creature contacted you. Its masters wished it to manipulate you."

I struggled for words. "But… why me?"

"It is simple. As an attendee at the party of a judge, you could be assumed to have more comprehensive knowledge of the Judiciary than the average ruanir. The reality that you are the granddaughter of a judge, the niece of another, and the child of a high-ranking member of our society would only have been more fortuitous for them. Beyond even that, however, you are a young woman who was all alone on the beach before the attack. You presented an easy target, one the dehaians could frighten into believing their monster had actually saved her life."

I bit my lip.

"You know the stories of what this creature did to our kind. Trust us when we say they do not compare to the horror of the truth. Our *one* defense has been our anonymity and now that is gone. The Beast came to find us and dehaians came with it. We cannot know how long we have till they attack again. And this time, the Beast will almost certainly be following new commands—ones which we will not survive."

I couldn't breathe. "What do you want from me?"

"Your help. You have been exposed to this creature's magic. Moreover, you bear its signature, and elements of this magic are still inside you." He paused and when he spoke again, his tone sounded almost gentle. "But it is poisoning you, Miss Moreau."

I trembled. No. God, no.

His impassive expression reasserted itself. "Our analysis of my questioning last night confirmed this to be true. This fact makes you a danger to any of our people who come near you—a magical Typhoid Mary, if you will. But even though this was undoubtedly part of the dehaians' plan, we have devised a way to use this to our advantage. We only ask that you help us for the sake of your kind."

I glanced back to Mom and Jace, my heart pounding. I felt fine. Stronger than I ever should have after something like last night.

And if Jace had taken in even a *shred* of the magic within me, I would have killed him.

I felt like throwing up. "How?"

"By allowing us to bind you to this Beast."

"*What?*" Jace protested.

An enforcer grabbed his arm when he started for me. I made a frantic motion for Jace to stop.

"This is *ocean magic*," Jace snapped. "We can't use it any-more. It'll kill her!"

"Your sister has already been exposed. The elements are

within her system and without intervention, they will do her irreparable harm. You know this. Every one of our people have seen the aftereffects of ocean poisoning. But we are highly experienced in the manipulation of magical elements within a person, Mister Moreau. Our actions will protect her from the contagions, while still allowing a connection to this creature."

"What kind of connection?" I asked faintly, fighting to keep my gaze from going to the enforcers.

Highly experienced in manipulating magical elements in people. Yeah, there was that.

Oh God, I didn't want to end up like a greliaran or one of the enforcers.

I couldn't stop shaking.

"Empathic, if all goes well," Judge Engle said. "It will feel what you feel. Be aware of your location and obey your commands. Our historical records show evidence that the creature was designed to be capable of this, and new evidence has come to light to prove that fact. You say the creature swore it did not work for the dehaians, but our sources have brought us reports to the contrary. The Beast is psychically connected to the King of Yvaria's lover. It is under her control."

I swallowed hard. The king's girlfriend. The weird look on Noah's face.

"However, you will disrupt this. Confuse the creature by providing interference to the signal coming from the Yvarian king's lover. Additionally, its human form seems to contain the creature. Reduce it from an insubstantial consciousness to a shape we can trap and control. Your job will be to stay strong against however it tries to fight you, and then draw it here. Get it to appear in human form so that we might subdue it before it realizes our plan."

My stomach twisted. "And then what happens?"

"We will purge the connection from your system." Judge Engle paused. "This is the best way we have to isolate the creature—*now*, before it can hurt anyone else, and without the risk that simply waiting for it to strike again would pose." He regarded me solemnly. "You have the potential to be either an asset or a liability to your people, Miss Moreau. Which will you choose?"

My heart was pounding so hard it hurt.

"Do this to someone else," Jace snapped. "One of you. The judges already know how to take in ocean magic without dying, so just—"

"The magic inside her is a specialized contagion, Mister Moreau," another one of the judges stated coldly, "not something to be handed about like a toy. The fact your sibling has survived lends credence to the idea that the dehaians intended her to do so. Somebody else—*including* ourselves—might not be as lucky."

At our silence, Judge Engle sighed. "This is our point entirely. The Beast has never left a single one of our kind alive. Yet Ariabella lives. She now has magic inside her that, if it came in uncontrolled contact with any of us, could destroy us without the dehaians lifting a finger. This is the most insidious type of plan." He looked back at me. "Simply using our own kind to eradicate us."

I shivered. "Could it have been an accident?"

His brow rose. "Would you have allowed yourself to absorb ocean magic, Miss Moreau?"

My racing heart found a way to pick up speed. I shook my head quickly. "No, of course not."

"Then that seems doubtful."

"You said it'll be confused by this connection thing," Jace cut in. "What if it tries to hurt her because of that?"

"She will be surrounded by judges and enforcers the entire time." Judge Engle leveled a serene look on Jace. "Trust us, Mister Moreau, the potential your sister possesses for us is beyond measure. We will not let her be harmed by this creature."

"What about us, though?" Mom tried. "Maybe she'll be safe, but she's bringing this Beast to her. What about the rest of us?"

Judge Engle regarded her calmly. "Your assistance will not be required. You and your son may return to your hotel to await the results of our efforts."

Blatant relief flashed across her face. In spite of my fear, a little sliver of hatred dug into me at the expression.

"I'm staying," Jace said.

"You are not necessary for this procedure."

"I don't care. I'm not leaving my—"

"Jace," I cut in quickly. The enforcers were looking restless. They didn't like him arguing with a judge. "Please."

"You said it'll feel what she feels," Jace snapped at Judge Engle, ignoring me. "You'll need someone to help her stay calm."

"The argument is valid," one of the female judges said before Judge Engle could speak.

Expressionless, Judge Engle glanced back. My gaze twitched to the woman nervously. I recognized her. Judge Irene Marseilles, Logan's mother. Dressed in a black pantsuit with her dark hair swept up in a tight bun and thinly rimmed glasses perched on her nose, the woman looked like an accountant from hell. She raised a perfectly plucked eyebrow at Judge Engle.

"Agreed," added another. "He is her brother. He will have more of an effect on the girl than anyone. His presence may be beneficial."

Judge Engle returned his attention to us. "Very well. The boy will stay." He paused. "*If* Miss Moreau has agreed to assist us?"

I looked between them. I wasn't sure about this. Noah… he hadn't *seemed* like he was trying to manipulate me. If anything, he acted like he'd wanted to get out of there as soon as possible.

Maybe he'd just been eager to get back and report on what he'd found. What he'd managed to do to me.

It hadn't seemed like that…

My heart pounded. I could have *killed* Jace. *Still* could.

All because Noah had done this to me.

"Eight people died last night," Judge Marseilles said. I blinked, trying to focus on her in the glare of the sunlight. "Murdered by dehaians. One of them was only fifteen years old."

My stomach became a ball of lead.

"You are our best chance to make certain this doesn't happen again," Judge Engle added.

I cleared my throat awkwardly. "What are you going to do to him?"

Judge Engle's brow drew down.

"*It*. I mean, it," I floundered. "What are you going to do to it? If I'm going to be connected to that… that creature…"

I couldn't meet his gaze. That wasn't the real reason for my question. It was just so hard to reconcile the boy I'd seen last night and this thing they described. It was hard to let go of thinking he'd saved my life. But if Noah really *was* under the control of the dehaian king's girlfriend, if he'd lied to me and done this to me on purpose…

He'd seemed so worried when he touched me.

Maybe he was just worried I'd die before I got back to the others.

"We will only do what is necessary to make certain the dehaians cannot harm our kind. On that, you have our word."

I hesitated. That wasn't really an answer.

"We have all done what we must to survive, Ariabella," Judge Engle told me quietly. "You know this. But if the dehaians come for us, if this creature is what we fear or what is inside of you begins to spread to others, then all our centuries of battling extinction will have been for nothing. Countless more will perish. Perhaps the ruanir will cease to exist entirely. We need you to be brave now, for all of us."

I shivered. My head moved in a stilted nod.

"You have the gratitude of the Judiciary." Judge Engle looked to the enforcers. "Return Madam Corvienne to her hotel and have the staff prepare a room for her son."

One of the enforcers nodded. Mom hurried after the man, not sparing us a glance.

Jace came up next to me, an expression on his face like he dared the judges to stop him.

Judge Engle ignored it. "Follow us," he said to me.

He walked toward an archway on the far end of the massive parlor. I could see stairs beyond it, but nothing else.

I trailed the judges from the room.

Narrow didn't begin to describe the confines of the staircase, and with judges ahead and enforcers behind, it took effort to keep myself breathing. At the lead, Judge Engle followed the twisting stairway down, passing blind corners and sconces glowing with gold light. Ahead of me, Jace glanced back, concern in his eyes.

I tried to give him a reassuring smile, though the expression couldn't quite compete with the butterflies chasing themselves dizzy inside.

We reached the basement level and Judge Engle left the stairs for the hall. Dark wood covered everything here, from the floors to the walls and ceiling, leaving me feeling as though we were walking through the root of a tree. At a door halfway down the hall, he stopped. He drew an old brass key from his pocket.

The key clunked in the lock. Judge Engle pushed back the

door. The other judges filed into the room and, nervously, I followed them to the doorway.

Half a dozen assistants waited in the room, men and women both among their number this time. More wood paneling surrounded them, along with glass-fronted display cases that lined the walls, all of which held bottles and vials filled with multicolored liquids and things I couldn't identify. A desk stood to one side, its top covered in tubes and beakers, while behind it, more panes of glass hung. Maps of North America were etched into them, while an opalescent sheen shifted and moved across the surface like it was alive.

My gaze flicked over it all, taking everything in, only to be brought to a stuttering halt by the object at the center of the room. A chair like the kind from a dentist's office but with straps on the arms and legs. The thing was made of dark leather and iron, and mostly reclined so that whoever was on it would be lying nearly flat under the bright overhead light.

My feet stopped. This was a bad idea. I couldn't do this. I was making a mistake.

Judge Engle caught sight of my expression. "I realize this must look intimidating, but please understand that it is only for your protection."

"You're going to strap her into that thing?" Jace demanded.

"For her protection," the judge repeated.

"But you're..." I swallowed, working to make my voice sound less faint. "I mean, this looks like *enforcer* stuff. I'm just going to, like, *connect* to the Beast. Not *become* it or something, right? Surely you don't have to—"

"I understand your trepidation," Judge Engle interjected. "But please try to see that while it may seem like overcompensation, this truly is to keep you safe. We are dealing with incredibly dangerous magic, Miss Moreau. It is vital you remain still during the procedure. If you should change position or flinch at the wrong moment…"

I nodded on autopilot. My gaze didn't leave the chair.

It took tremendous effort to make my feet move. On unsteady legs, I crossed the room. Cold leather chilled my back through my shirt when I sat down. Two of the assistants set to strapping down my ankles while two others took my wrists.

My heart raced. This was *such* a bad idea. I'd never *had* such a bad idea. But if I hurt anyone with this ocean magic inside me, if the dehaians actually were starting up their war again…

People could die. My people. Maia. Dhanya. Jace. I couldn't let that happen.

I drew a deep breath, struggling to calm down.

"Now," Judge Engle said while a redheaded woman brought over a syringe filled with strange green liquid. "This will help you remain relaxed."

I watched the woman nervously. She ignored me. With meticulous gestures, she swabbed the inside of my arm with frigid alcohol and then lifted the syringe. I winced when the needle bit into my skin.

Pressure built at the spot where the needle rested in my arm. I concentrated on continuing to breathe.

A second slid past. The strangest feeling began to spread through me, like the rock-solid connection to my body had suddenly come loose. My awareness of my arms and legs, of the straps over them, faded into nothing. My racing heart slowed till every beat felt centuries apart. The light fragmented gradually around me, scattering and drifting apart and turning to rainbows as if I was viewing the room through a kaleidoscope of cut glass.

Judge Engle appeared near my feet. Jace was a blur by the door, though I could feel his eyes locked on me.

The judge lifted a hand. A twinge of fear stabbed through the haze inside me. I remembered this. It wasn't good. I didn't want to feel him doing this to—

A wet, cold blanket of magic engulfed me. Drown me. I felt like I'd been plunged into swamp water. Like my throat was full of algae and slime. I choked on the air, trying to breathe around it, while my body lurched in a desperate attempt to escape the feeling.

The sensation grew worse. Stronger. I heard someone shouting, the sound far away, and then I realized it was me.

And Jace. He was struggling to reach me. The enforcers were holding him back. I gasped, trying to tell him to stop fighting. They would hurt him.

I couldn't do anything.

Other judges appeared. Their hands rose and blackness swallowed me before I could make a sound. And I couldn't breathe. Couldn't see. Everything was the dark, deathly magic of the judges and in it, I was dying.

A new sensation joined the first. Bright enough to hurt, sharp enough to sting. It surfaced inside me like a rope of light and I scrambled after it, latching onto the new presence like a lifeline.

It was a mistake.

White-hot fire exploded through me. I screamed, my body arching in the restraints, while everything inside me burned to nothing, leaving only an ashen darkness that took the world away.

## 6

# NOAH

The guest rooms in the palace easily dwarfed any hotel room on land, with ceilings at least twenty-five feet high and arched windows that extended most of that length. Bowls of opaque glass hung from the dark stone of the ceiling, with impossible flames burning inside.

"So…" Chloe said nervously, watching me while I glanced around. "This is it. Seem okay to you?"

I tried not to look at the soldiers hovering by the door. "Yeah."

Chloe's smile was strained. Her gaze twitched toward them and away.

I turned back to the room. She'd been struggling to keep up a pretense like this was normal the whole way down here. Like she couldn't see how the other dehaians stared or how some of them had fled in terror when their friends whispered who I was. Shouts and cries had echoed from deeper in the palace halls, and I thought I'd seen a few of the servants faint when I'd glanced their way. Rumor obviously traveled fast around the palace, helped along by the fact some of the soldiers clearly had spread the word that the Beast had returned.

It made it even harder to want to stay. Most everyone I knew among the Yvarians wasn't here. Zeke's sister Ina was in someplace called Teariad with her boyfriend, according to Chloe, and Zeke's grandfather Jirral was off on a diplomatic mission beyond the Yvarian border. And besides Zeke and Chloe, that brought an end to the list of potentially friendly faces, leaving me only with the ones that were filled with fear.

"I was thinking we could do a dinner tonight," Chloe offered. "Invite a few of the ambassadors and give them a chance to meet you. Kind of ease them into thinking you're not out to kill us, that sort of thing."

I hesitated. It sounded horrible, but only on a personal level. "Yeah, okay." I paused. "You've become quite the diplomat."

She blinked, discomfort flashing over her face.

"I didn't mean that as an insult," I amended quickly.

She hesitated and then gave a small nod.

"It'd probably help," I continued. "As long as they don't think I'm working for Yvaria or—"

A cold shudder ran through me.

My brow furrowed in alarm. I barely felt cold anymore. Or heat. I hadn't for a year.

"Noah?" Chloe asked, swimming closer. "Are you okay?"

I shook my head. "I—"

It grew worse. So much worse. Pain and fear came too, cascading at me like water pouring down a chute, and I choked on it.

But this wasn't from me. This was like Chloe. Like Baylie. An awareness of location, of wellbeing.

Of *extreme* pain.

My eyes widening, I looked to Chloe. "Baylie."

"What—"

I didn't wait. I let my human form vanish and raced for the window. I could hear the soldiers shouting, hear Chloe trying to calm them while calling to me, but then the mountain was at my back and the veil around it was too. In a heartbeat, I sped beyond the city and took to the open water.

Whatever was hurting Baylie was going to *die*.

I shuddered, fighting the cold-hot rage straining to break free inside. I didn't know what was happening to my stepsister, didn't know who was hurting her or why, but I wouldn't lose control. No matter what was going on here, I would *not* lose control.

Innocents could be killed if I did.

I raced onward, but the seafloor wouldn't end. The miles were taking too long. An eternity passed before the water began to grow shallower, and amid it all, a thousand scenarios raced through my mind, each worse than the one before.

But Baylie would be fine. She *would*. I'd stay calm, I'd find her, and—

The pain vanished.

I slammed to a stop, shock radiating through me. It was gone. All of it, like a faucet turned off. Panic surged inside me. I raced upward through the water and into the sky.

Nothing. Absolutely nothing. But California lay on the

horizon ahead. Struggling to keep control, I sped toward it.

I couldn't let myself become the Beast's other form up here. Not yet. To say that roiling, black nightmare of a thunderstorm was too noticeable was a ridiculous understatement, and if Baylie was in trouble, stealth was my best asset right now.

California came closer. Baylie's presence surfaced in my mind, like a cool blue glow that I could feel more than see. There wasn't any pain, though. No fear. Nothing like what had been pounding through me only minutes ago.

Crossing over the coastline, I veered toward her. Downtown Santa Lucina passed beneath me, with its shops and restaurants and tourist traps. I slowed and then dropped lower till I reached a small alley behind the main strip.

Everything condensed. I glanced around, making sure no one had noticed me, and then jogged toward the street.

At the corner of the alley, I paused. She was there, across the road from me. She seemed strangely different in a way I couldn't quite place, though that was probably just a side effect of the fact it'd been so long since I'd last seen her. She sat outside a café, her blonde hair shining in the sunlight, and she sipped a coffee while tapping something one-handedly into her purple-cased laptop.

I scanned the street. Besides a couple college guys checking her out while they walked by, I barely saw anyone glance her way.

This wasn't right…

Her brow furrowed. Looking up from her computer, she turned her head toward me.

Cursing, I ducked backward into the shadows of the alley. The connection worked both ways. She'd picked up on the fact I was here.

I glanced around. Something like what I'd felt earlier wouldn't just vanish, and yet from everything I could tell, Baylie was fine.

And starting to head over here.

I scowled. This wasn't how I'd wanted to see her after a year of being gone. After what I'd just felt, I was shaken and barely in control. Holding onto human form was harder than it'd been for months. And meanwhile, whatever the hell I'd felt was still out there. I couldn't just stop and—

It came back. I choked, my hand bracing me on the brick wall. The fear surged and the pain did too. But it wasn't Baylie. I could feel her and she was fine, albeit coming closer with every second.

I vanished and raced upward. This was coming from farther east. A *lot* farther. But Chloe was behind me, Baylie was here, and—

No.

No *way*. I'd been careful. The freak accident that had connected the three of us to the Beast before I'd become this had been just that. An *accident*. A damn near nuclear explosion of magic that had leveled the forest around it.

I'd only picked Ari *up*.

"Noah?" Baylie called. "Is… is that you?"

She was in the alley, looking around with an expression like she was really concerned people would think she was insane for talking to the sky.

I retreated higher, hating myself as I went. I should go to her. This was pathetic. Yes, everything sucked, but now I'd left my stepsister standing in an alleyway looking like a lunatic.

The feeling of fear grew stronger, along with the oddest sense of questioning, like Baylie wasn't the only one calling my name. It was timid, though, and so very, very frightened.

And the pain wasn't gone either. It tugged at me, making me desperate to have it stop.

Dammit, I'd be back. I just needed to figure out what the hell was going on. And *carefully*, because this shouldn't have happened and, since it involved wizards, it was probably a trap.

Snarling curses to myself, I headed east.

## 7

## ARI

Everything was agony when I opened my eyes, like my whole body had been run over by a steamroller and then skinned alive for good measure. My neck and face were wet with tears I didn't remember crying. My throat was raw and my heart raced. Something was wrong. Had gone wrong. The judges hadn't said anything about pain.

And so much of it. My entire body was shaking. I couldn't make it stop.

"Did it work?"

Judge Engle's voice came from a million miles away, but it dug like a weevil into my ears and I wanted to scream at the feeling.

"The alterations have been made. Stage one is complete."

Confusion moved through me at the assistant's voice. Alterations? Stage one?

"Ari?"

Jace appeared over me. His hands hovered above my shoulders like he was afraid to touch me.

I shook my head, the motion short and jerky. It hurt too much. Everything hurt too much.

"What the hell did you do to her?" he yelled at someone I couldn't see.

I gasped, closing my eyes and trying to pull away. It was excruciating, the shout. It felt like a bullhorn blasting through my mind.

"Miss Moreau."

I opened my eyes. Judge Engle was above me now.

"Focus, Miss Moreau. Focus on the Beast."

Fresh tears poured down. What had they done to me?

"Focus and the pain will stop."

My breath hitched. I didn't know how to do what he said. Focus on the Beast? How would that—

I froze, my eyes widening. I could feel him inside my head, like a strange, gray presence far in the distance. A storm on the furthest edge of the horizon, churning with rage.

He was terrifying.

"Call to him, Miss Moreau."

I shook my head. This wasn't like the magic I could feel on land, slow and steady and so incredibly old. This was a hurricane and it would eat me whole.

"You must."

A choked sob left me. Shaking my head again, I closed my eyes. I wanted this gone. This wasn't part of the plan. This pain. This fear.

This *monster* inside my mind.

Judge Engle said something in a low murmur. I couldn't

make out the words.

"Ari?"

Jace's voice. I looked up, finding him.

His gray eyes were pleading. "Ari, just do it. Get it over with. They say it'll stop hurting then. Please."

The expression on his face hurt for a whole new reason. I didn't want him to be in pain, to be scared. I drew in a stuttering breath. Yeah. Do it and make this end.

My gaze fell away from Jace's. I took another breath, this one steadier.

In my mind, I called Noah's name.

He heard me. Terror spiked when I felt the ominous weight of his attention focus on me. I looked back up at the judge.

"Keep calling, Miss Moreau. You will hurt less the closer the creature comes."

I shook my head.

"Keep calling."

I said Noah's name in my mind again.

Anger. Frustration. And then a sense that he was heading my way.

I gasped.

"Sir."

At the sound of the assistant's voice, I turned my gaze toward the far side of the room.

"It's coming," the woman said.

She nodded to the glass map of North America on the wall behind her. A blue-green glow was moving on it, like a strange blush of light.

"How long?" Judge Engle asked.

"A few hours?" the woman offered.

He looked back to me. Tears burned in my eyes. I shook my head again, pleading with him silently. I didn't want to wait hours for this to be over. I just wanted the pain to stop.

His mouth tightened. "Take her upstairs. Have her ready for when it arrives."

The enforcers came toward me. Air burned my skin when the straps were taken away.

"Can you move?" one of them asked.

The question held more accusation than concern. I shuddered. The pain was lessening—only a bit, but still. The judge had been right.

Trembling, I moved to stand.

My bones felt as fragile as cracking glass. I gasped.

Jace hurried over. "Stay still." He scooped me into his arms. "Just breathe."

I choked, wanting to beg him not to touch me. His arms hurt. Everything hurt. And I didn't want him to be exposed to this too.

I couldn't make a sound.

Carefully, he carried me toward the door.

I felt every slight adjustment, every impact of his feet on the ground, and they threatened to shake me apart. Closing my eyes, I focused as hard as I could on drawing in air while Jace continued through the house.

Warmth burned my skin. I opened my eyes. We were outside.

"Set her over there." Judge Engle pointed to a wooden bench at the center of a large garden in the yard. Gravel pathways twisted through the whole place, all of them trimmed with green stones stained by moisture and algae. Strong trellises surrounded the garden, with long poles arching between their tops over the entire space. Flowering vines tangled along the piping overhead and filled the air with their scent, while birdhouses hung amid the blossoms. Cheeping noises came from inside.

It was like being enclosed in a botanical dreamland.

Jace brought me to the bench and lowered me down. He glanced darkly to the judges and enforcers who stayed by the house.

"What… what is it?" I whispered hoarsely.

"Nothing."

"Jace."

"They didn't say a word about this *hurting* you."

I swallowed hard, trying to get my voice back. "Maybe they didn't know."

He met my gaze flatly. I looked away. I knew it was stupid, defending them about that. They were judges; magic was their specialty, more than any of us.

But Judge Engle had promised the only point of this was to help our people. To keep the dehaians and the Beast from attacking us. And he'd said they were doing this to help me too. So surely they would have warned me if they'd known how this was going to feel. Surely they wouldn't have—

"Is that thing still coming?" Jace asked.

I hesitated and then gave a small nod. I could feel Noah's location, just like they'd said I would.

He felt like a nightmare barreling down on us.

Shivering, I tried to concentrate on anything else.

A minute crept by. Birds chirped and flitted between the birdhouses. A bee hummed around the flowers overhead, investigating them methodically.

"Do you think this is hurting him?" I whispered.

Jace glanced to me, that dark look back on his face. "Feel what you feel."

I swallowed again. It still had to be a mistake. This much pain *had* to be a mistake.

"Ari," Jace said, his voice so soft, I could barely hear him. "When that thing shows up, I'm getting you out of here."

I stared at him.

"They lied to us. They said this was about bringing it here, capturing it, but they didn't say a word about pain or what happened in that basement."

I trembled, not wanting to think of how that might've looked to him or how it'd felt at the time.

"What if this is about more than what they claimed?" Jace pressed quietly. "What if they're going to try to control that thing and *this* is how they plan to do it?" His jaw muscles clenched. "Hurting you. *Torturing* you, just so that it'll feel pain too. What happens if they…"

He didn't finish. I felt sick.

"I'm getting you out of here," he repeated.

"But then who's going to fix this?"

He didn't respond.

"Jace, I can't stay like this. I've got ocean magic in me. It—"

"I know."

The words were sharp. I looked away.

"We can share it."

I turned back to him, my eyes wide.

"They'll take care of the Beast," he said, "and we'll run like hell. I can take some of the magic from you. Slow the poisoning down."

"Jace, no. You just went through the adjustment. You barely—"

"We'll find someone to help us. Someone who doesn't work for the judges."

"There *isn't* anyone who—"

"Joseph."

Pain pressed on my chest. "He's dead. The… the Beast, he—"

"It killed him?"

I shook my head. "No. Greliarans did. They—"

"And you believe that?"

I searched for a response and couldn't find one. "We have to stay."

He dropped his gaze to his hands, saying nothing.

I closed my eyes, wishing Noah would get here faster so this could be over. Meanwhile, though, the pain was better. Judge Engle hadn't been wrong about that, at least. My body wasn't shaking as horribly and I could breathe without worrying I was going to choke. My mind still felt stretched and unsteady from this sudden awareness of something outside myself, but the agony of it was lessening.

Time passed. Servants brought the judges iced tea while the assistants returned to the house. The enforcers never moved, leaning against the pillars of the broad porch like they had been carved there.

And then the Beast came over the horizon.

My breath caught.

"What?" Jace asked.

"He's close."

I looked back at the judges. Reading the expression on my face, Judge Engle straightened in his chair, setting his drink aside. His hand twitched at the enforcers.

They left the porch, circling toward the far ends of the property and the trees there. The other judges disappeared into the house.

"What are they doing?" I asked.

"Just stay calm," Jace told me, taking my hand. His gaze darted over them all like he was searching for an escape route. "Remember what I said."

I drew a breath, not sure how we could do what he'd argued. The enforcers were all around us. We'd never stand a chance of getting away.

And that was without Noah closing in overhead.

My gaze twitched toward the sky. He was almost on top of us. I could feel caution radiating off of him in waves, along with a sort of angry certainty, like he knew this was a trap.

"Miss Moreau."

I flinched and glanced back. Judge Engle was walking toward me. All the other judges were gone.

"Ask it to meet you down here," he said. "But walk back to me. Mister Moreau, stay there. Do not let the creature come too close to your sister. It may attempt to kill her in an effort to break the connection."

I stared at Judge Engle in alarm. Jace couldn't stop this thing.

"Ari," Jace whispered. "Go. No matter what happens, do like I said."

I turned to him, disbelieving. His eyebrows rose pleadingly, tension in the lines of his face.

My gaze slid toward the blue sky past the twisting flower vines. "Noah?"

He was there. I knew it.

I inched my feet back, retreating toward the judge outside the gazebo. "Please?"

He dove toward us.

I gasped. Jace backpedaled as black clouds erupted from nothing, all of them racing down like a fist from the sky.

And then the storm hit us and Noah didn't stop. Jace shouted and crashed into me. The ground disappeared. With all my might, I hung onto my brother.

The air turned to lightning.

I screamed. Pain surged, but it wasn't me. It was Noah. I could feel it, the electricity ripping into him, tearing through him and racing toward us. The pain of it was blinding. Agonized, he faltered. We started to fall.

A growl tore the air, like thunder all around me.

Noah caught us. Wind howled in my ears. It wasn't like last time. Sharp-edged and fierce, the velocity of the wind scathed my skin. I squeezed my eyes shut and clung to Jace.

As quickly as we rose, we began to drop again. Ground thudded into us. Hard.

I choked, rolling away from Jace and fighting to bring air into my lungs. My eyes opened. Blue sky above me. Ragged grass below. A wall of trees not too far away on any side.

I felt Noah nearby. All the emotion and agony rushed toward a center, like an explosion in reverse.

He appeared only a few yards from me.

And then he staggered and dropped to his knees, catching himself with his hands.

"Ari," Jace groaned.

I looked to him. Scrapes and scratches covered him. Pain etched his face when he pushed away from the ground.

His strength gave out. He collapsed back onto the grass.

I couldn't breathe. That much ocean magic. Contact with me. With Noah. He'd just gotten through the adjustment and he was drained as hell. If he'd absorbed any of it…

I didn't think. I just reached out, my hand landing on his arm.

Swiftly, I drew it in. Jace cried out in protest and struggled to get away from me.

The magic had already transferred. A weird buzz sizzled through my veins, cold and yet fiery.

I let out a breath. It didn't hurt, though. Not like it had.

But maybe I was already so poisoned, it didn't matter

anymore.

I tried to sit up.

"Ari," Jace gasped. "Damn you, what—"

"Won't let you die," I rasped.

"What about *you*?"

I couldn't look at him. It was done. Protectiveness was a two-way street.

Pushing to my feet, I stumbled toward Noah.

"Ari!" Jace protested.

I didn't look back. On his hands and knees, Noah shuddered. Waves of rage poured off of him, slamming into my mind like the ocean against a seawall. I put my hands to my head, barely able to breathe from the assault.

"What the *fuck* did you people *do* to me?" Noah snarled.

His gaze snapped up to mine. I stopped. His eyes were completely black. Electricity crackled across them like lightning in a night sky.

"Please," I whispered. "Please, I didn't—"

"You're willing to *die* to kill me?"

I stared at him. I didn't want to die. I wanted this gone, all of it. I wanted the judges to take what Noah had done to me away.

He seemed to feel my confusion. The rage pulled back. Just a bit, but enough that I could breathe.

"I helped you," he growled.

"You tried to kill us."

The confusion came from him this time.

"Ocean magic," I said. "From you. It contaminated me

and—"

The anger returned. "I didn't do *anything* like that." He shuddered. "Do you have any idea how *careful* I was? How much I held back to keep from hurting you?"

Exasperation and fury buffeted me and it was hard to argue with them. He meant it. Whatever had happened, he hadn't—

A horrible new possibility occurred to me and my blood went cold. I'd been terrified. I'd been drained. Magic had surrounded me and in all my disorientation and fear…

"Oh God," I whispered.

The blackness faded from Noah's gaze. Still shaking, he watched me.

I looked back to Jace. He was eyeing Noah like, Beast or not, he'd take the guy on if he came near me.

"It wasn't him," I said. "Not on purpose. It really must have been me. I… I must have done it by accident." I turned to Noah. "They said it was all your plan from the beginning. That you'd gone back to report on your mission and that everything on the beach was just a setup. They said they knew the dehaians had ordered you to infect us all—"

"*Infect* you?"

"Magic from the ocean. It's toxic to us. And if one of us has that magic in us and we share our energy with another who shares it with another… it's like a disease. It could kill all of us."

Noah eyed me up and down. "You seem to be doing alright."

I shivered. "Takes time."

Radiating disgust, he pushed to his feet. I retreated a step.

"I didn't do *any* of that," he growled, straightening. "Yeah,

I went back to the dehaians, but to do *exactly* what I told you: check to see if they'd been the ones who came after your people. Their king swears he wasn't."

Jace scoffed. "And we're just supposed to take your word for that?"

Noah's eyes became darkness again. "You *really* don't want to mess with me right now."

I moved fast, putting myself between them. Noah's gaze went to me. A heartbeat passed before the blackness faded.

"They told us the king's girlfriend controls you," I said carefully.

He stared at me, silent for a moment. "No."

The word was flat. Emphatic. I trembled.

Noah shook his head. "So you heard this and thought… what? You'd let them kill you instead?"

"They weren't going to—"

"That thing you were in? With the flowers and green rocks? The whole place was wired. Lit up like a hell of magic and lightning when I came into it. They may not have planned to kill you, but I notice he wasn't retreating." He jerked his chin toward Jace without taking his eyes from me. "If I hadn't gotten him out of there, he would have cooked."

Jace muttered a curse. I looked back at him.

He met my gaze levelly.

Air pressed from my chest. I felt like sitting down again.

Help them, they'd said. Jace could help them. He'd have an effect on me.

Oh my *God*…

Noah made a noise of discomfort. I turned to find him glaring at me, a hand to his head like it hurt. "What did you let them do to you? *Us?*"

"I'm sorry." I cleared my throat, fighting to speak when all I wanted to do was scream. "It wasn't supposed to be like this. At least, I didn't know it would be. They only said you'd feel what I felt. Know where I was. That sort of thing."

"No kidding."

He grimaced. I felt something shove at my mind like a wall.

And it hurt. My vision swirling, I stumbled.

"Hey!" Jace snapped, catching me.

The feeling lessened. Breathing hard, I pushed away from Jace again.

"Listen," I said to Noah, my voice choked. "I get that it's weird, alright? Having more than a single person connected like this to you now. I didn't—"

Caution and confusion came at me in equal measure and I cut off.

"What?" I asked. "What is it?"

He paused. "Nothing."

I could tell he was lying. "But you—"

That wall came at me again, stronger than before and filled with a strange anger that seemed driven by fear. I cried out, staggering away while pain crashed into me like I'd run head-on into bricks.

"Stop it, damn you!" Jace yelled.

The feeling retreated like a watchdog only half-convinced its enemy was gone.

"How do you make this go away?" Noah demanded.

I floundered, still fighting to catch my breath. "T-the judges were going to break the connection once they—"

Noah scoffed. "Right."

"I don't *know*, okay? They lied. It was only supposed to let you know where I was so that you'd come find me—"

"So they could kill me. And him."

I hesitated. "Capture. They didn't mention the other part."

He regarded me dryly and it hurt to feel the contempt coming off of him. He thought I was an idiot. He sort of, pretty much hated me.

I struggled to push back against it. I didn't want that in my head.

He winced. The intensity of the feelings reduced.

"Who else can fix this?" he growled.

"I'm not sure."

He turned away as if to leave.

"Don't go," I said hurriedly.

He looked back.

"Please. It hurts if you're too far away from—" I cut off, trying to regroup. I doubted he cared that the distance was painful for me. But that also wasn't the only problem. "The judges… they can track you."

He stared at me.

"In your other form. When you're like this, they lose you. But the Beast… that invisible magic part of what you do… they can detect it whenever you're not deep underwater. They've been watching you for the past year."

He turned away. I felt something furious coming off him, like he was swearing internally.

"I don't know who can help us, okay?" I continued. "I wish I did. But no one will go against them, not when it's obvious the judges have done this. They're the leaders of our people. There isn't a ruanir alive who would question them. And as for what the judges did…" I trailed off, wanting to cry or swear and not really being sure which first. "They have a different kind of magic than us. More powerful. More… more *horrible*. There isn't anyone I know who could overcome it."

"What is it?" he asked, not looking toward me.

I shivered at the memories. "It's land energy corrupted by ocean magic. The judges change themselves to contain the ocean's power, so they can drain it from any of us who encounter it. That's what they do. They protect us from the ocean, from each other, from humans. They make themselves impartial to any emotion or compassion, so that they can't be accused of favoring one of us over another. But everything they do comes at a cost. A terrible cost. And one of those costs is that their magic… their magic feels like death."

His gaze slid back to me and for a moment, he didn't say anything. "Do you think they can track you? Since… whatever you let them do."

I shook my head. "I don't know. I think it's only you in your other, you know, form."

He scowled.

I looked to Jace. We needed a plan. Ocean magic or no ocean magic, this was going to hurt me if something wasn't done.

And that didn't even bring into it this connection thing still beating at my head.

"Can these judges pick up on dehaians or landwalkers?" Noah asked.

I paused. "They didn't say that and… I mean, I've never heard of the judges monitoring their kinds. But dehaians just deal in ocean magic and landwalkers don't have any at all. How could they help?"

Noah stared at me. "You guys missed that?"

"Missed what?"

He hesitated. I could feel distrust take the place of his surprise.

"Nothing," he said. "Never mind." He glanced around the clearing. "The landwalkers might not have magic like you understand it, but they still may be able to help and right now, that's all we've got. So come on." He grimaced. "I think I saw a town that way."

Leaving us to follow, he headed south.

"Ari…" Jace began.

I gave him a helpless look. "What else is there?"

He hesitated and then sighed, shaking his head. He motioned for me to go on.

Together, we started after Noah.

## 8

# NOAH

The girl's emotions pounded against my head, a thousand times stronger than Chloe's or Baylie's had ever been. I'd never picked up much of what those two were feeling—not more than a gist, anyway. Enough to know they were alright. Enough to know if they needed help.

It was nothing like this.

My leg passed through a stand of tall grass and I scowled, fighting to keep my body together. Everything in me felt on the verge of flying apart, like the lightning and wind of the Beast's other form were churning madly beneath my skin. I couldn't lose control, though. Not now. If those bastards could track me…

She could be lying. This could be another trick.

I glanced back at her darkly. Lying or not, she wasn't handling whatever they'd done to her very well. Snow pale with dark circles under her eyes, she could barely keep her feet. The guy with her was watching her as much as me, with a look on his face like he expected her to fall over at any moment.

It was obvious who he was. His hair and eyes were the exact same shade as hers, and his features were similar as well. He was a little over half a foot taller than Ari and looked several years older too, but he eyed her with a protectiveness that just screamed brother.

I turned back to the path ahead, dismissing him from attention. I didn't *think* she was lying. She'd felt like she believed it when she said these judge people could track me. She'd seemed terrified of them, though less so than of me.

Though why the hell she would have let them do *this* to her…

That weird sensation pushed at my mind again. She'd felt that thought. I snarled under my breath, fighting back.

"Dammit!" the guy snapped at me.

I looked back to see Ari stumble. It felt alien to care. There was too much anger in the way. I knew I should. I wasn't a monster—at least not that kind. But right now, with how fuck-ing *furious* I was at how she'd helped those people almost capture me, with how much I wanted to make those people pay—

Grimacing, I fought against that too. I needed to… something. Calm down. That.

I stopped walking. My eyes closed. I wouldn't be like this. Inhuman. A mad creature of rage. I hadn't been as a greliaran and I refused to be now. So I *wouldn't* lose control of this. Me. The blind fury that the Beast was capable of terrified me. I had memories of it, horrible images of fire and lightning and death that floated up like misty snapshots from before its centuries of sleep. I didn't want to think of what could happen if I ever gave in to that. So I had to stay calm. I couldn't let those ruanir bastards have a chance to find me again.

Find *us*.

The anger cooled, self-preservation kicking in. The Beast side of me understood self-preservation. It'd survived all this time on the basis of that drive alone. These judges had connected Ari to me for a reason, and I doubted it was *only* to bring me into their little cage. Her pain and emotions ricocheted around in my head now, almost like they were happening to me too, and if those freaks hurt her…

A shudder ran through me at the idea.

"Are you okay?" I heard her brother ask.

I glanced back again. She nodded at him.

"Whatever the hell you're doing, just quit!" the brother snapped at me. "She's not your enemy."

I eyed him and then looked to her. I could feel something under her pain and fear, and it made me pause.

It seemed like desperation, pushed too far and out of options. Like anger that didn't know what to do.

I studied her. She was one of these wizards. She'd set me up.

And I'd met her for all of ten seconds. I was the Beast, the creature that—if her expressions on the beach had been any indication—the ruanir were still petrified of after all this time. The leaders of her people had sworn I'd set *her* up. That I was trying to kill her friends and family with some weird, ocean-magic-disease thing.

That I was still a slave to the dehaians.

And yes, I'd told her that wasn't true, but again, I was the

Beast. These were the leaders of her own people. Who was she more likely to believe?

I grimaced. I had no reason to trust her and about a million reasons not to.

Except she was in my head now, and the dumbstruck horror that had come off her when she'd found out they could've killed her brother…

I dropped my gaze to the grass and weeds, trying to concentrate. I'd never been overwhelmed by Chloe or Baylie. Maybe there was something to that. Some way I could use my familiarity with *that* kind of connection to distance us and keep us from being so affected by each—

She shrieked and crumpled to the ground.

Pain and shock reverberated through me. I rushed over to her, ignoring how the grass stalks passed through my legs.

Her hands were clutched to her temples. She was shaking.

"What the hell did you do to her?" her brother yelled.

I dropped down beside her. "Ari." I took her shoulder, trying to pull her back upright.

Something tugged at me, like the tiniest amount of the storm inside me was drawn away.

Into her.

She gasped. The pain faded.

Breathing hard, she looked up at me. "What did you do?"

I shook my head. I felt fine—better, actually, than I'd felt since she let them do this to her—and the aching sense of her in my mind had lessened as well.

"It doesn't hurt as much," she whispered.

On autopilot, I nodded.

Her brow furrowing, she dropped her gaze from mine. She pushed to her feet.

I didn't let go of her. "Are you okay to walk?"

She nodded. "I-I think so."

I took my hand from her shoulder. The pain didn't return.

Keeping an eye to Ari, I started toward the road again. She followed, warily staying close to my side.

"So, um," she began after a moment passed. "I guess… introductions, right?" She glanced over. "Jace." She twitched her head to me. "Noah. Noah, Jace. He's, um, my brother."

The guy glared like he was a heartbeat from ordering me away from his sister. I continued walking. I could feel the discomfort coming off Ari in waves.

"How far away is the town?" she asked me.

"Not sure."

"Okay, well…" She looked to her brother. "Do you have your cell phone? I left mine at the hotel but maybe if you called someone, they could meet us in town?"

Jace reached for his pocket and drew out the phone.

The screen flickered to life in a fragmented confetti of scattered pixels and then died.

Jace swore. "Great. You killed it." He glared at me.

"Or the judges' thing did," Ari interjected hurriedly, as if feeling the anger coming off of me. What would he have preferred? I let him fry?

Jace shoved the phone back into his pocket and continued on. Ari remained between us, radiating discomfort like a pulsating light.

It was distracting.

The clearing gave way to a road and I couldn't focus enough to bring my feet to make sounds on the gravel. A breeze tumbled through the warm summer day, passing through me as much as over my skin.

She'd said she absorbed ocean magic from me. That she'd started this off by accident. And that'd been weird enough. But when I'd touched her shoulder… it felt different. It felt like she'd needed something from me, an energy more than the specific kind of ocean magic I lived off of.

What the hell had they *done* to her?

"So these people you want to go meet?" Ari tried. "Where are they?"

"Colorado."

"*Who* are they?" Jace asked, his voice harder than Ari's careful tone.

I glanced to him. "Elders. Landwalker leaders. I know one who lives there."

And I hoped like hell Olivia could do something about this, even if I didn't have a clue what that'd be.

"You know landwalker elders," Jace said, as if the words confirmed some crime I'd committed.

I kept walking.

"How are we going to get there?" Ari asked. "Do you know someone who can come pick us up?"

I didn't respond. To be honest, I wasn't entirely certain. I hoped Ari or Jace had money, and I hoped this town had a bus or train station—or at least that we could find a cab to get us closer to either. But beyond that, I didn't really know.

I missed flying already.

"You don't have any idea, do you?" Jace said.

"If you have a suggestion, I'm happy to hear it," I snapped.

He glanced to Ari questioningly.

"Mom'll turn us over to the judges," she said.

A weird twist of resentment came off of her as she spoke.

"Maia," Jace said.

A spike of fear went through Ari. "Uncle John," she said as if countering the suggestion.

"He's in Australia. Hasn't even spoken to her in a year."

Ari's fear took a darker turn. "Dhanya's whole extended family, then."

Jace paused. "She'll go along with it for Maia."

Ari went quiet. Worry emanated from her like ripples on the surface of a pond. I tried to keep from putting a hand to my head at the emotional roller coaster.

"Maia?" I asked. "Like last time?"

She nodded.

I hesitated. This was awkward. "She going to send a limo again? Because that's not exactly subtle."

Ari looked to me. "You were watching."

She didn't feel shocked. Not entirely. More like I'd confirmed something.

I tried to bury my discomfort in the hope she wouldn't notice it. "Dehaians could have shown up."

Ari paused. Something weird followed my words, like

thoughtfulness and uncertainty combined, but I couldn't quite catch all of it before it was gone. She shook her head. "The limo was from my mom."

"And this Dhanya person or Uncle John?" I asked.

The discomfort came from her this time. "Dhanya is Maia's fiancée. She, um, she'll be fine."

My brow climbed. She didn't exactly sound confident about that.

Ari shrugged anxiously. "A lot of her extended family are enforcers. Sort of these, um, people who work for the judges. But Dhanya… she won't…"

"And Uncle John?" I demanded when she trailed off.

"Maia's father. He's a judge."

Ari winced at my alarm. Were they nuts? They couldn't seriously want to *trust* these people?

Jace looked annoyed at both of us. "We don't have any choice."

"And if they turn us over to the judges?" I argued.

"Maia and Dhanya wouldn't," Ari insisted.

"The judges still might be watching them."

Jace looked away. Ari's worry pushed at me, stronger than before.

I grimaced. If I was still capable of getting a migraine, this would make it happen.

They didn't say anything more while we kept walking. The road looped around a gradual curve, and the trees obscured the view beyond. When we passed the turn, I spotted gas station signs in the distance, tall enough to tower above the trees. They gave me hope that the town ahead was larger than I'd thought. I hadn't seen much of the place when we'd passed over it earlier. I'd been too distracted by pain. A vague sense of buildings and a road large enough to be a highway were the only things that had made an impression.

I still had no idea what to do once we got to town.

Scowling, I pushed the thought away.

Time passed with the warm summer wind and the glare of the sunlight. Houses started to crop up between the trees, along with small businesses with a few cars speckling their parking lots. Every window felt like it held someone watching us and each motion from the corner of my eye just made me miss the three-hundred-sixty-degree awareness of the Beast more.

Up ahead, the end of the long stretch of road came into view. A whisper of noise cut through the air, growing louder the farther we walked.

The street dumped us into a commercial district that the trees had thoroughly hidden from view. The interstate lay a quarter mile beyond that, with an enormous gas station occupying a frontage road beside it. A small collection of fast food places and convenience stores peppered the remaining space around the highway.

But no matter how far we walked, there weren't any signs of busses. No trains either. And besides the commercial area we'd passed, the rest of the town didn't seem large enough to warrant a stoplight, let alone taxis.

I grimaced, glancing to the others.

"Maia's the only one who'd risk helping us," Jace said to Ari, who was watching the highway traffic. "And Dhanya will be trustworthy, if only for her sake."

"I don't want them to hurt her or Dhanya, though."

"Me either. But you've got to get this thing fixed, and if Colorado is the place that can happen…"

She swallowed hard. "Okay." She glanced to me. "Payphone again, huh?"

I wasn't sure what to say. It felt like déjà vu, only everything had gone to hell this time around.

We walked toward the gas station. Car fumes and the smell of greasy food hung on the air, and people's voices carried from the parking lots, their words distorted by the distance. The station itself was massive, one of those truck stops that looked like a landing pad of cement with a one-story building at its heart. Semis fringed the lot, while cars crowded closer to the pumps near the door, and the sunlight glared from both. There wasn't a payphone outside the station though. Reluctantly, we all headed past the vehicles and into the building.

A blast of air conditioning hit us and a ding rang from the door. My gaze darted around fast. Security cameras dotted the walls, their glassy eyes locked on every aisle. Behind the register, the cashier barely glanced up, while deep into the junk food section of the store, a pair of teenagers examined the selection, ignoring us.

It didn't matter. Nervousness thrummed through me, born of the fear that I'd draw any attention to what I was. I'd avoided people for so long for a reason, and that was before what these judges had done. The last thing I wanted was to give even the slightest sign I wasn't human while surrounded by people and security cameras.

"What is it?" Ari whispered to me.

I shook my head. "Nothing."

We walked up to the counter. I eyed the cashier and the store around me while Jace asked for change.

The cashier never looked my way.

We walked to the payphone in the far corner. Jace handed Ari the change. She picked up the receiver, inserted the money, and then dialed the number.

Seconds passed.

"Maia? Hey. Look, something's come up. I need your help again." She paused, glancing around the station, but no one seemed close enough to hear her. "It's the judges. Jace and I are in trouble with them. It's complicated to explain, but we ran from them and now we're stranded. I know it's asking a lot, but is there any chance you could come meet us and maybe help us get a car to—"

She cut off. "Oh." She covered the receiver with her hand, looking to Jace. "They're already at O'Hare. Their plane landed in Chicago a few minutes ago."

He muttered a curse.

Ari took her hand from the phone as if Maia had said something. "What?" She paused. "No, if you come back, they'll know you're helping us. Look, we're pretty sure they'll be watching our accounts but if we could just get a credit card number from you, we could try to— what?"

A sinking feeling ran through her. She looked to Jace again.

"They already got a call from her father about us."

Jace scowled like he was swearing much more vehemently inside. "The Judiciary will be watching them then. And their accounts. They're probably watching anyone we know too."

I glanced between them, incredulous. How much of a reach did these judges have?

"Listen," Ari tried, returning to the call. "Don't worry about us. We'll just—" She cut off. "Maia, you don't have to—" She bit her lip briefly. "Is Dhanya alright with that?" She nodded at whatever she was hearing, though the worry didn't leave her eyes. "Okay, but Maia, we really don't want to put you in danger. If they—" Ari winced, looking grateful and pained at the same time. "Thank you. Please be careful."

She hung up the phone. She glanced back to her brother. "They want us to try to meet them in Chicago. They're going to drive us wherever we need to go."

Jace let out a slow breath, looking to the window and the tiny town outside.

"You sure you trust them?" I asked.

Ari turned to me, certainty in her eyes. "Maia's like a sister to us."

I didn't respond and she looked away sharply, her face tight. I could feel her worry, no matter how sure she claimed to be.

"Come on," Jace said.

He started for the door and Ari hurried to catch up. I went after them.

"What?" I asked when we came outside.

He glanced to the gas station behind us as if checking no

one could hear. "Truckers. We see if they'll give us a ride."

Ari cast a quick look to the semis. "You think they will?"

Jace shrugged.

"We'll need a cover story," I pointed out.

He eyed me briefly and then looked away, thinking. "Dad," he said to Ari. "We'll say we're going to visit him in the hospital, but our mom hates him. Doesn't want us to go. We'll claim this guy's a friend helping us."

Jace twitched his head toward me.

"No time to get bags," Ari agreed, though I could feel her nervousness pushing at me. "Total emergency."

"We can't use our names, though," Jace said.

Ari bit her lip.

"So who do you want to be?" I asked dryly.

He ignored my tone. "John works." He raised an eyebrow at Ari.

"Belle?" she suggested.

They glanced to me. My dad's name would do. "Peter."

Jace nodded. We headed for the semi.

The engine started even as we were walking toward it. Jace jogged a few steps to reach the window before the driver took off.

"Hey!" he called.

The driver looked down from the window at us.

"We're wondering if you could give us a lift. It's an emergency."

The man shook his head. "Sorry, man. Company policy. If I take extra passengers, I could get fired." He put the truck into gear. "Good luck."

We stepped back. The truck pulled away in a cloud of exhaust and dirt.

"What's the emergency?"

I turned toward the semi behind us, a massive thing of glistening green with a sleeping area and a curtained porthole of a window. The trailer behind it was white and I didn't recognize the logo of the company on the side. A weathered old woman leaned out of the passenger window. Her skin was browned from the sun and wrinkled, and she wore a denim shirt without sleeves. Her bright blue eyes were cautiously curious as she waited for our answer.

"My dad," Ari said. "He's in the hospital. We're trying to reach him."

"Don't you kids have a car?"

Ari shook her head. "Just my mom's, but she hates him. Rather he died."

The woman regarded us silently. I glanced to Ari. That last hadn't exactly felt like a lie.

"Can you help us?" Jace asked.

She looked to the station. A man with a cowboy hat was walking toward us, two bottles of an energy drink and some beef jerky in his hands. His steps slowed when he spotted us and his brow furrowed with curiosity.

"What's this, Rhonda?" he asked, coming up to the trailer.

"Kids need a lift to see their dad in the hospital."

He eyed us up and down. "Hard to bring three of you."

Anxiety shot through Ari. My jaw tightened.

"Squeeze them in back?" Rhonda suggested, her tone neutral.

The man's mouth thinned. "Where ya'll headed?"

Jace glanced to Ari. "Far west as you'll take us."

A heartbeat passed. The man glanced toward the station.

"Yeah, alright. Hurry up."

He jerked his chin toward the semi. Rhonda pushed open the door and then moved out of the way.

Ari scrambled up after Jace into the truck. I could feel the man's eyes on us while I followed.

The inside was like an apartment squeezed into a space barely larger than a small bathroom. A bunk took up the rear wall, while a microwave and a short refrigerator occupied the passenger side. A storage closet faced them, leaving enough room to stand and move around a bit, but not much else. The air was thick with the stale smell of cigarettes; several extra packs were stuffed into the space between the microwave and the wall.

We took a seat on the green blanket of the bunk. The man walked around to the other side of the vehicle and climbed in.

He shut the door with a thud. "Okay, well. This is Rhonda." He nodded to the woman. "I'm Ted."

Jace glanced to his sister. "I'm John. This is Belle and that's Peter."

The man nodded. "Nice to meet you. We can get you to Toledo, leave you someplace you'll probably find another truck to take you farther."

"That'd be great," Jace said. "Thanks."

Ted nodded again. He put the truck into gear and gravity rocked us when the semi started out of the parking space.

We left the gas station behind.

# 9

## ARI

We rode with Ted and Rhonda for hours, long into the night. They traded off, one resting in the passenger seat while the other drove. I figured one of them would normally take the bunk and sleep, but with the three of us around, they were more liable to want to stay conscious and cautious.

Not that I felt like much of a threat. I doubted any of my magic had survived what the judges had done to me, and Jace's was almost certainly still gone after his adjustment. But then, if anything went wrong, Noah would probably destroy everything in the cabin and the entire truck besides. So there was that.

Maybe they were right to be cautious.

I pushed the thought away. We had just as much reason to be paranoid. But meanwhile, I ached from the day, a throbbing exhaustion that only became worse as time crept on. Leaning against the wall on the opposite side of Jace, Noah didn't seem like he felt much better. Sitting between us with his elbows braced on his knees, Jace had been keeping up the

129

flow of conversation for hours, following along as best he could with topics ranging from sports to food to whatever questions Rhonda or Ted asked. But even he was starting to look drained from it all.

And what we'd do once we reached Toledo was anybody's guess.

I grimaced, leaning back against the pillow.

"You okay?" Noah asked quietly.

I looked over to him. His brow twitched up.

"Yeah."

He nodded, his gaze returning to the wall of the storage compartment beside the bunk and whatever it was he saw there. It didn't really seem like he was watching it.

"You?" I whispered.

A heartbeat passed. "Yeah."

It felt like he was lying. His green eyes were dark, more so than they should have been even in the dim golden glow of the bunk light overhead, and strain showed in the tight lines of his face.

Worry moved through me. If he lost control here or if they saw what he could look like…

I hesitated. He'd helped me earlier today. He'd touched my shoulder and I'd felt something leave him, like a wisp of magic that'd dulled the pain I'd felt. It didn't make sense—this poisoning should be making me feel worse, not better—but it'd happened.

Maybe he needed help too.

I reached out and my fingers brushed his arm. His skin was

cool, inhumanly so. When I touched it, I let a bit of magic pass to him.

Beneath my fingertips, his skin warmed.

He jerked away, alarmed. "What are you doing?" he demanded in a whisper.

Jace glanced back, floundering in the middle of his response to another of Rhonda's questions.

I dropped my gaze away, not answering. There'd been a chance this would bring back the pain or that it'd make this poisoning worse. But instead, I just felt strange. Achy, but not in the same way as before. More stable too, like I wasn't going to collapse as easily. The exhaustion had dulled as well.

"*Belle?*" Noah hissed.

I looked back to him. "Did it help?"

Irritation came off him in waves, pushing at me. "Yes, but you can't—" He grimaced. "What hurts you hurts me too. If you—"

"It doesn't hurt."

Frustration tinged the pressure. He looked away.

Quiet returned between us.

"Toledo exit coming up," Ted called back.

Jace cut off his conversation with Rhonda.

"We can drop you all off at a truck stop there," Ted told us. "Might be hard to get a ride so late, but come tomorrow morning you should have more luck."

"Thanks," Jace said.

Ted nodded. The semi slowed. The bright glare of the truck stop lights burned my eyes when we drove closer. I winced, looking away.

The truck rolled to a halt. Rhonda opened the door and climbed out so that we could leave.

"You kids take care," she said.

I smiled.

"Thanks again," Jace told her.

She got back in. We walked toward the truck stop. Behind us, the door slammed and then the semi rolled away.

I glanced around the parking lot. Most of the semis were dark, and some had curtains drawn over their windows. The truck stop itself was blinding even at this late hour. Past windows that made it seem like a fishbowl, I could see an empty restaurant.

"Now what?" Noah asked, scanning the lot as well.

Jace stifled a yawn.

"Inside?" I suggested.

Noah nodded. We headed toward the restaurant. Golden light surrounded us when we came past the doors, the glow emanating from hanging fixtures above maroon-upholstered chairs and booths. Warily, we glanced around, but no one came to welcome us or ask us what we were doing there. There weren't even customers inside.

Still eyeing the restaurant, we walked to the far corner, where Jace sank into a booth. I sat down next to him while Noah took the opposite side. Leaning against the wall, Jace sighed.

"Damn, that was a long trip," he said.

I didn't respond and Noah didn't either. We were only in Toledo. The distance from here to Chicago felt like a million miles.

And that didn't bring into it how far we had to go from there.

Jace shifted against the wall, not saying anything else. On the other side of the table, Noah regarded the restaurant. We were still alone, with no sign of a hostess or waiter. I was glad. I was hungry, but I sort of hoped they'd stay away and maybe give us a chance to rest.

Next to me, Jace let out a breath. I glanced to him. His eyes were drifting closed.

"I can wake you up if anyone comes over," Noah offered quietly.

I looked back. He shrugged.

"Do you sleep?" I asked, suddenly curious.

He hesitated. Everything between us was uncomfortable now, even more so than I suspected it would've been without this connection. It was like having someone looking over your shoulder all the time.

"I rest," Noah allowed. "But not like that."

He twitched his chin toward Jace.

My brow rose questioningly.

"It's like what you saw," he said.

"The invisibility thing."

He nodded.

I paused, thinking about it. "You were a greliaran before this."

Confusion followed my words.

"Is that weird?" I continued. "Like, I mean…" My gaze skimmed across him. I couldn't find the words to explain.

He looked away. A moment passed. "It's all weird."

Nothing more followed.

"I'm sorry," I said. "For letting them do this to me. To us. For agreeing to it. Just… everything. I'm sorry."

He was silent for a heartbeat, and then he shrugged again. "They're the leaders of your people. I'm the Beast. Makes sense who you believed."

I blinked, taken back by the words. By their kindness.

"Why 'Belle'?" he asked.

I hesitated, trying to regroup. "Just part of my name, the full one. Ariabella Celestina Moreau." His brow twitched up and I shrugged. "Mom's desperate for us to be aristocrats. I prefer Ari."

He paused. "Noah Delaney," he said. "Not an aristocrat either."

My lip rose in a small smile.

"And your dad?" he asked. "I'm guessing he's not in a hospital?"

I shifted position uncomfortably. "He died. About three years ago. Car accident."

"I'm sorry."

I nodded. "Do you have family? I mean, like, greliaran family, or…"

He was quiet. It almost felt as if he was weighing whether to trust me. "Yeah," he allowed finally. "Brother, dad, stepmom, stepsister, all that. They're in California. Mom's in Kansas."

My brow rose. "Wow. I guess being, you know, *this*, you save on airline tickets, right?" I tried for a smile.

Discomfort rose in him, killing my attempt at humor. "I haven't been to see them. Not since…"

I waited, but nothing more came. "Why?" I risked asking.

The discomfort strengthened. "Not really something I want to talk about."

"Sorry."

He shook his head dismissively.

A moment crept by. I skimmed my gaze around the restaurant, uncertain what to say.

"So back in the truck," he began, as if trying to change the subject. "What did you do? When you—" He made a tiny motion toward my hands.

"We share magic," I said, my gaze flicking around again out of habit. No one was nearby to hear. "I thought, after how you helped me, maybe you needed some help as well."

He didn't respond.

"Why was your skin so cold?" I asked.

He hesitated. "It always is."

I paused at the words. At the discomfort in them, and the strange, jumbled emotion that lay beneath it. My hand reached out toward his.

He pulled away. "I take magic from things," he said softly. "You can't—"

"So do we. And we share it. And apparently so do you."

Caution radiated from him. I moved my fingers closer.

My hand wrapped around his. He was chilly like fog. I couldn't feel a pulse at all.

I drew a breath. Magic flowed out of me into him and my

fingers tightened on him when he tried to pull away. Anger flashed through him and then his opposite hand moved fast, taking mine.

The draining changed. Stabilized. Magic flowed back to me through his other hand, cycling around and around till I lost any sense of the cycle at all.

Pain faded. The ache had gone on so long today that I'd forgotten what the alternative felt like. An odd sense of peace settled in its place, like something that'd been off-kilter inside me had suddenly righted.

Beneath my fingertips, his skin warmed, becoming human.

I looked up at him.

Noah was watching our hands. I felt his surprise, followed by a flare of horrible sadness that he smothered only a second after I realized it was there. He moved to let go.

I tightened my hold. "Is it enough?"

Shock shot through him. He yanked his hands away like I'd burned him.

"What?" I asked.

He shook his head. "Nothing."

His tone was hard. I stared at him, confused.

"I should go find us another ride." He pushed away from the booth seat.

"Noah, *what*?"

He stopped. I couldn't get a handle on what was coming from him. The tangle of it was overwhelming.

"Don't try that again," he ordered shortly.

And he walked out of the restaurant.

## ❧ 10 ❧

## NOAH

I was halfway around the side of the building before my feet slowed, and if I'd still had a heart, I was fairly certain it would have been pounding.

I'd panicked. I shouldn't have, but that didn't change anything. I'd never experienced something like that in the entire time since I'd become the Beast. It wasn't like in the truck. That'd just been a whisper.

But *this*…

My eyes squeezed shut. I'd felt human. Real. Normal again like the past year hadn't happened and I'd just been an ordinary guy sitting at a table rather than a sentient thunderstorm clinging by its fingernails to self-control. And it'd hurt, that sudden awareness of what normal *actually* felt like. Of how different I'd become. I hadn't realized how much of it I'd forgotten.

And when she'd asked if it was enough…

I scowled, opening my eyes again. It was stupid. I *knew* it was stupid. I wasn't hung up on Chloe anymore and hearing her words repeated back to me… it shouldn't matter. And as for bringing back the memory of that day on the beach, of my first few moments as the Beast when I'd taken what she could do and spread that through all the dehaians and landwalkers, just so I stood a chance at survival…

Or the memory of the way Chloe had trusted me to do it, when at any moment the Beast could have killed her…

I scrubbed a hand over my face and then froze at how much warmer and more solid my skin seemed compared to before. Those memories shouldn't matter. And this weird effect would fade. The parallels to that day were nothing and…

And I could have killed Ari too.

I leaned against the wall. I didn't think she realized it; she hadn't seemed scared. But I'd felt it when she first took my hand. Something was different about her. I could pick up on the magic in her now in a way I hadn't before. In a heartbeat, I could have taken that and done away with this connection between us entirely. It might have killed us both.

Or maybe only her.

A shudder ran through me. The Beast side of me had gone eerily quiet, but I doubted even it wanted to do that anymore. I didn't know *what* it wanted. What *I* wanted. And this…

I hated that it would go away.

My shoulders shifted against the rough wall. That wasn't true. The temptation to disappear into the sky and pretend this hadn't happened was overwhelming. It's not like I'd *wanted* to feel like this. Like a ghost who'd been given a glimpse of what it was like to be alive again.

It only made everything harder.

And it wouldn't be forever. The whisper of a difference I'd felt when she touched my arm in the truck had vanished in only a few minutes. So this would fade, and I'd forget, and it'd be fine. I'd continue on through this lifetime and the next and all the ones after that and this wouldn't be a problem. After a while, the memory of what a real body felt like wouldn't even matter anymore.

I'd have centuries to prove *that* true.

A sensation moved through me, almost like my stomach twisting, and I grimaced. The sooner this went away, the better. Even if I'd been having trouble in the truck, even if hanging onto human form was getting harder the farther from the ocean we traveled and left me feeling weaker besides, it was still preferable to this.

*Anything* was preferable to this.

A semi pulled in and came to a stop in the shadows at the far end of the parking lot. I shoved away from the wall and strode toward it. Based on what Ari had started to tell me in the field earlier, I knew that putting too much distance between us would hurt her, but she seemed okay for the moment. And I'd told her I was going to find us another ride. I might as well give that a shot.

Inside the restaurant, I felt her moving away from the booth and toward me—curiosity and concern coming from her, but not pain.

I walked faster.

"Hey," I called to the trucker when he climbed out.

He looked over. He was easily the size of a large football

player, with a stained blue t-shirt stretched over his muscles and ragged jeans that had obviously seen better years.

"Any chance you could give me and my friends a ride?" I asked.

He eyed me briefly, the dismissal in his expression making clear he was about to say no.

I felt Ari coming up behind me.

The man's gaze twitched toward her. I saw something flicker through his eyes, cold and hungry and then gone. He started to nod. "Well, yeah, I think I could—"

"Never mind," I cut in quickly.

I backtracked, not looking away from him.

"Um, Peter?" Ari said as she walked up to me. "The waiter told me we can't stay in the—"

"Hey there," the man called to her. He strolled closer, glancing around the empty parking lot. "You need a lift?"

"No," I countered before she could respond. "We're good." I put a hand to my pocket. "Yep, cell phone's buzzing. That's probably John now. Thanks anyway."

I twitched my head at Ari, motioning her toward the truck stop.

"Now where are you going to find a ride at this time of night?" the man pressed, continuing toward her. "Hell, you could be out here for *days* looking for somebody to help you. There's no telling what kind of people you could end up with."

He reached for Ari. I stepped between them quickly.

"Don't," I warned. "Just leave us alone."

"I'm only trying to help you out, kid." He wasn't even

looking at me. His gaze just skimmed over Ari like he was shearing off her clothes with his eyes. A lascivious smile twitched his mouth. "No need to get riled up."

The Beast stopped being quiet in my head. I heard it snarling. It wasn't mad at her anymore, but it was damn well *furious* at what this man wanted. Ari was *ours*. Under our protection. Like me. But not like me. Something new and he couldn't have her.

The thoughts tumbled through my mind. I didn't have time to question them.

"Come on, girl." The man tried to step around me. "What's your name? I'm sure we can help each other out here."

My eyes went black. I grabbed his arm.

"Hey!" He moved to push me aside, and then caught sight of my eyes. "What the f—"

I shoved him. He flew back and slammed into the side of his truck.

"Stay away from her," I growled.

The guy staggered up, blood dripping from a gash on his head. Staring at me, he retreated to the door of his truck and scrambled inside. The truck jolted and then the engine roared when he floored the pedal.

In a screech of gears and pistons, the semi raced from the parking lot.

Shudders ran through me while my gaze tracked the vehicle, daring it to slow down.

"You guys alright?" Jace called. "What the hell happened?"

I glanced back to see him jogging toward us. A plastic bag

was tucked under his arm.

"Guy tried to grab me," Ari said, sounding breathless. "Noah stopped him. Emphatically."

"Oh." Jace hesitated. "Thanks."

His tone was shocked. I ignored it, scanning the truck stop and hoping not to see any cameras pointed our direction.

"They're all focused on the pumps," Jace said. "Angles aren't right to catch anything out here."

I turned back to him.

His brow twitched up. "You think we don't watch for cameras too?"

Without waiting for a response, he pulled the bag from under his arm. "Since they kicked us out, I grabbed a few things. Thought maybe we could find a place out here till morning."

Ari took the bag. Jace eyed me briefly and then nodded for me to follow when he started away from the truck stop with his sister.

I hesitated, feeling like I'd passed some kind of test with him. Maybe not all of them, but one. I wasn't sure I cared, except that not getting glared at like a monster all the time would be nice.

Though that was still probably asking too much.

I pushed the thought aside and fell in behind Ari and Jace. I couldn't make sense of what had raced through my head when that man had reached for her. Ari was a ruanir and a girl who'd made a mistake in trusting the asshole leaders of her people. I wasn't sure she'd even qualify as a *friend*, and she sure as hell didn't *belong* to me. That was psychotic. But there was also something off about her, something that'd been changed by what those judges did to her. Something that felt like it was still changing even now.

But she *couldn't* be like me. It wasn't possible.

The Beast side of me had gone quiet again. It wasn't sure about this, though—about any of it—that much I could tell. It only knew she *was* changing. Becoming something else, even if it didn't seem like it on the outside.

And I had no idea what that could mean.

❧ 11 ❧

## ARI

We spent the night near a stand of trees half a mile from the truck stop. With a little of his cash, Jace had bought a few blankets which served as places to lie down, and after a fair amount of fidgeting and itching, I'd finally managed to drift off to sleep with him a safe distance from me. Noah remained sitting by another tree several yards away, keeping watch.

My dreams were nothing but nightmares, however. Blurred, terrifying images of death and fire and people screaming, and when I woke, I almost wished I hadn't tried to sleep at all. For his part, Noah appeared drained when I opened my eyes, like he'd endured every minute of those dreams. He didn't say a word to me, though, and when we finally found a trucker willing to give us a ride, he never even looked my way while he climbed into the vehicle.

I couldn't figure out what I was picking up from him. Emotions churned through him like tumbling clouds, appearing and then vanishing into the mix before I could get a handle on what I'd felt. I knew I'd upset him with what I'd tried yesterday, though I didn't understand why. But ever since that man had tried to grab me, the swirling mess of emotions coming from Noah had gotten even worse than before.

It was making my head hurt.

Rubbing my temple, I looked out the front window of the semi. We were rolling in toward a truck stop in Gary, Indiana where the driver had agreed to drop us off. A while before, we'd used the man's cell phone to call Maia and tell her where to meet us. With any luck, she'd already be waiting when we arrived.

With no luck at all, the enforcers and judges would have already found out about this and they'd be the ones waiting instead.

Maybe it wasn't just Noah giving me a headache.

"Hey," Jace said quietly. I glanced to him. He gave me an encouraging smile, not needing this screwed-up connection Noah and I shared to know how I was feeling. I could see the same anxiety in his eyes. Maia's father was a judge. Dhanya's extended family was practically made up of enforcers. So many things could go wrong here.

Jace's brow rose, silently insistent. I struggled to smile in return.

The driver slowed the semi and then turned into the truck entrance. I craned my neck, trying to get a better view through the windshield. Like every other truck stop I'd seen, the main building was half convenience store and half restaurant. There weren't too many cars around this one—just a few midday travelers and some semis stopped farther away.

And Maia's SUV.

I swallowed hard, my stomach churning with nervous energy. The silver luxury SUV sat next to the main building. Behind the smoked windows, I could just make out two shadowy forms that I prayed were Maia and Dhanya.

The truck pulled to a halt. The driver glanced back to us after putting it into park.

"Thanks for the ride," Jace said.

The man nodded. Jace handed him the money that we'd finally had to promise someone just to get them to give us a lift. We climbed out.

Warm wind swept around me, carrying exhaust from the semis and grit from the empty lots beside the truck stop. The road nearby was under construction—a mess of orange barricades and enormous, yellow equipment—and the chomping sounds of the machines tearing through the concrete drowned everything. With Jace beside me and Noah a step behind, I started for the SUV.

The door opened. Maia got out, relief on her face. On the other side, Dhanya climbed from the vehicle.

I started breathing again. We hurried toward them.

"Did anyone follow you?" Jace asked when we came close.

Maia shook her head. "I don't think so. We were careful. Gave the neighbors a cover story of going to visit her sister and tell her about our engagement." She nodded toward Dhanya. "But guys, what *happened*? My dad wouldn't be clear about it. Why would the Judiciary have a problem with you?"

I wasn't sure where to begin. "Long story. But, um, listen,

you don't need to drive us. If we could just borrow—"

"And what?" Maia protested. "Leave you guys on the run? Ari…" She looked at me like I was nuts.

"You're family," Dhanya said firmly. "You're in trouble. We want to help."

I hesitated, watching her. No matter what I'd told Noah, Dhanya still worried me. I'd known her since she and Maia started dating two years ago and she seemed like a wonderful person, but that didn't mean I could trust she'd go up against the Judiciary for me.

I wouldn't trust almost *anyone* to do that.

Her dark eyes were like iron, though.

Maia took Dhanya's hand, nodding. "Just tell us what's going on."

I didn't know what to say.

"We need to go," Noah urged in a low voice.

Dhanya studied him briefly. "Who's this?" she asked, her tone becoming cagey.

"A… a friend. It's kind of hard to explain." I glanced to Noah. "This is Maia Davenport. Dhanya Singh." I motioned quickly in introduction. "Guys, this is—"

Tires screeched. Maia's expression transformed with shock. Dhanya's eyes went wide.

I looked behind me. Three sedans rushed into the parking lot.

They headed straight for us.

"Go!" Jace shouted.

We scrambled for the SUV. I tumbled into the back, narrowly

avoiding landing on Jace, while Noah jumped in behind me. Maia threw the gear into reverse and sent the vehicle flying backward. I fumbled for the seatbelt while she yanked the gearshift around. The SUV roared forward.

The sedans moved to cut us off.

Maia swore desperately.

"Go right!" Dhanya shouted.

Maia gasped and hauled the wheel sideways. The SUV charged up onto the sidewalk and narrowly missed the concrete pillars designed to protect the station there. People stumbled back from the entrance, shouting. The enforcers swerved, trying to get in front of us again.

Our SUV raced past them, darting through the lanes between the pumps. I spun, looking out the rear window.

The sedans whipped around, coming right after us.

A panicked sound left Maia and immediately, I could see the problem. We were on the far side of the lot from the interstate. The only way to reach it was past them.

In other words, we had no chance in hell.

The curb arrived and the SUV bounced over it hard. Pulling on the wheel, Maia steered us in a tight curve around the construction crew, leaving the workers shouting in her wake. An intersection flashed by and then rundown houses followed, their yards big and overgrown and containing nothing to help us at all. We flew past a stop sign, sending another car screeching to a halt, and Maia veered wildly around a beat-up truck creeping down the road ahead of us.

Horn honks followed, fading into the distance fast. I

couldn't see the interstate anymore. Even crossroads seemed to disappear as the edge of town fell behind us and left only cornfields.

But the sedans hadn't stopped. They were getting closer.

"What now?" Maia cried.

I looked to Jace.

Staring out the back window, Dhanya spat something in Hindi and it sounded like swearing. I turned.

An enforcer was climbing from the car like a stuntman, pushing up through the sedan's sunroof and bracing himself on the metal.

"What the *hell*?" Noah protested.

"Faster!" Jace yelled.

Maia made a frantic noise. "We're going as fast as we—"

The enforcer leapt through the air and slammed down onto the SUV. The roof crunched toward us. Maia shouted, swerving hard.

Glass shattered, raining from the sunroof. The enforcer lunged down.

Noah exploded into wind. He surged toward the enforcer, ripping him away from us and up through the gaping sunroof. I whirled back to see the man sail into the sky, rising higher and higher for a moment only to be flung hard toward the ground from a hundred feet above.

Blackness swirled like the ghost of a thunderstorm forming from the clear blue sky, and then I felt Noah rushing down. The clouds slammed into the sedans, scattering them like bowling pins and sending them flying into the fields around us. In twisted piles of metal and glass, they tumbled to a stop. No one moved inside.

"Maia!"

I turned back at Dhanya's cry. Maia slammed on the brakes, bringing us to a fast halt, and then her hand fumbled at the handle. Shoving the door aside, she tumbled from the SUV.

Dhanya scrambled out of the vehicle. Frantically, I followed.

Maia was on the ground. Shrieks escaped her, agonized, and she lurched like she was being stabbed. Her body curled into a fetal position. On her neck, her skin was turning green and black; the stain was creeping toward her face.

I couldn't breathe. This wasn't happening. I wanted to wake up now.

Jace moved fast, grabbing Dhanya when she raced toward her fiancée. "No!" she shrieked, struggling against him, fighting to reach Maia.

I felt Noah appear behind me, an explosion in reverse that was filled with shock.

"What happened?" he demanded.

I couldn't find the words.

"He must have touched her," Jace explained, his voice choked. In his arms, Dhanya was sobbing, her expression every bit as tortured as Maia's. "Enforcers poison people. Magically poison them. We can't… if you touch her, it'll kill you too."

I could feel Noah's horror.

Maia spasmed. Dhanya gave a desperate cry. Tears in my eyes, I turned away, unable to watch.

Noah strode past me, every other emotion vanishing into

rage.

Jace made a protesting noise. "What are you—"

Noah dropped to his knees beside Maia and clasped her arms. She shrieked in pain.

And then I did as well.

I felt the magic rush into Noah, through him, and my legs gave out, sending me to the ground. It burned, the poison. The scathing, horrible, deadly poison that snapped and lunged at me as though it wanted to devour me alive.

But it didn't.

A ragged breath entered my lungs. The magic twisted and thrashed like a trapped snake, but with every heartbeat the pain reduced as if something was drawing it away.

Neutralizing it. Deadening it. Absorbing and changing it into something else.

Gasping, I opened my eyes. My hands were braced on the gravel roadside. My whole body burned as though I'd stayed too long in the sun. Several feet away, Noah shuddered hard and then released Maia's arms.

He turned back to me. In his eyes, I could see swirls of black fading. "You alright?"

I couldn't stop shaking, but I nodded.

He echoed the motion. Pushing up from the ground, he retreated from Maia.

The black and green had vanished from her skin. She seemed barely conscious, but her breathing became easier and easier with every moment.

Noah looked to Dhanya. "Poison's gone."

A cry left her. She broke free of Jace and rushed to Maia. Falling to her knees, Dhanya pulled Maia into her arms, tears running down her cheeks. Weakly, Maia reached over, her fingers clutching Dhanya's side.

"It's okay, baby," Dhanya told her, swiping the dark strands of Maia's hair from her face. "You're okay." She held her for another moment before she looked up at Noah. "What *are* you?"

Noah paused. "Complicated."

Dhanya studied him briefly and then nodded, accepting the answer. "Thank you."

She bent over Maia again, whispering assurances to her.

Jace came over while I climbed to my feet. "You sure you're alright?"

"Yeah."

He hesitated, seeming like he wanted to put an arm around me. I tensed, backing away for his safety.

Jace's jaw tightened. He gave a short nod, and then glanced to the others. Several feet away, Noah stood watching Maia and Dhanya.

"Thank you," I said to him.

Noah glanced to me. "I didn't hurt anyone, did I? With—" He jerked his chin toward the SUV.

I looked to Jace, who shook his head. "I don't think so," he said.

Noah nodded. "What the hell were those things?"

I hesitated. "Enforcers. Weapons of the judges. They carry out the judges' orders and make sure no ruanir endangers the rest of us."

"And they're poisonous?"

I gave a helpless shrug. "Yeah."

He stared at me.

"It's sort of like the greliarans," I tried, "except that greli-arans were too obvious, with the whole rock-and-fire skin thing. Enforcers aren't as much. But it's the same principle."

His expression hadn't changed.

"The judges can do that, you know?" I managed. "Change people to make them into things? The enforcers are stronger and faster than anyone but a dehaian, and yeah, poisonous but in a different way than ocean magic. More like… like venom. They can hurt with it, kill with it, whatever they're told to do. They're kind of like the judges too. Impartial. Cold. Except enforcers don't remember their lives before they became what they are."

Noah was silent for a moment. "They don't remember who they were?" he asked, a weird note in his voice.

"It's an effect of the process they go through. It's really sup-posed to be for the good of the ruanir, though."

His brow rose.

I grimaced. "Things got ugly after the dehaian war. Our people turned on each other. Formed factions. They even used humanity's paranoia of anyone who's different to manipulate them into attacking other ruanir. It was bad. There were blood feuds. Witch hunts. People burned alive—innocent humans too. We almost wiped ourselves out. So our ancestors decided impartiality was best. Leaders who would come to unanimous decisions and judge the same whether it was their child or someone who had once been their worst enemy. And weapons who could enforce those decisions and who'd be even *more* incapable of nepotism or partiality because everything that might cause them to act that way would be gone."

Discomfort twisted in Noah. "And do they become that willingly?"

My brow furrowed. His gaze darted toward the wreckage and the body lying in the field several hundred feet away. His discomfort grew stronger.

And the reason clicked. At least, I thought it did. "Yeah, they volunteer. It's considered an elite calling to serve as an enforcer. There's a big event about once a year where the ones who've chosen to become that celebrate with their families before they undergo the process. They know what'll happen, that they'll lose their memories and personality and everything, but they still do it. They want to be exactly what they are."

He looked back at me and I knew he could tell the words were the truth. The discomfort changed.

"Your world is really messed up," he said quietly.

I blinked. I'd never thought that, not once. It was just normal. Just what was.

And it would have killed my cousin today. It would have killed my brother yesterday. It had tortured me. Lied to me. Manipulated and used me.

All to capture the guy who'd saved my life.

Unease moved through me. My gaze went to Dhanya. Maia was awake and they were talking, their voices too low to hear.

"Yeah," I admitted. "You might be right."

It took Maia several minutes to be able to stand and when she did, there was no discussion of her returning to the driver's seat. With a glance to Jace, Dhanya led her to the back while he headed for the wheel.

I followed them, climbing in after Maia and keeping my distance from them both. Noah joined Jace up front, murmuring a city name as a rough direction of where to go. Silently, Jace nodded and then put the SUV into gear. Cops would be coming, or else people who would stop and call them. Either way, we needed to be gone when that happened.

We left the wreckage of the enforcers' cars behind.

"You okay?" Maia asked me.

I looked over to her and then jerked away when she reached for my hand.

Confusion filled her expression.

"Don't," I said, my heart pounding. She had to be drained after what happened. From the way the diamond bracelet on Dhanya's wrist was steadily becoming duller, I could tell Dhanya was giving whatever magic she had to help Maia recover. I couldn't risk whatever was in me getting through to them.

"What's wrong?" Maia asked.

Dhanya's arm tightened on her, pulling Maia closer and away from me. "What did the judges do to you?"

I glanced to Noah. He turned toward us slightly, listening, and I could feel his caution.

"That's what this is, right?" Dhanya pressed. "They did something?"

I managed a nod. "Yeah, they, um… they changed me. And they lied. About a lot of things." I motioned to the front. "This is Noah. He's not a threat to us. He saved our lives today, and he's saved my life repeatedly over this past week." I hesitated. "He's also the Beast."

Maia blinked, her gaze darting from me to Noah. "What?"

"It's a long story. But Noah's the reason I ended up in Massachusetts the other day. He saved me from the dehaians. He's not controlled by them. It got complicated, though. I absorbed some magic from him. I didn't know I'd done it at the time. But the judges said he'd poisoned me intentionally. They convinced me to help them capture him. They changed me. Connected me to him so he'd feel what I felt and vice versa. It's a, um, a thing Noah can do. They said it'd help them catch him." I paused. "They almost killed us instead."

Dhanya exhaled, looking away with a flabbergasted expression.

"Are you going to be okay?" Maia asked.

I nodded. "I think so. That's why we're going to Colorado. There are people there who might help us."

Maia stared at me, her eyes wide with worry and horror.

"I'm fine," I assured her. "It's actually getting better than it was."

She didn't look convinced. "Why are you back?" she asked Noah.

He shifted position on the seat and I could just *tell* he didn't want to get into it.

"Like I said," I told her. "Long story. I haven't heard all of it, but he's not here to hurt us. That I do know."

Dhanya nodded, her hand rubbing Maia's shoulder. "Yeah."

Noah turned back to the window. The SUV rolled on in silence.

Hours crept by, bringing sunset and then darkness that felt like it would never end. Sleep pulled at me, interrupted by passing headlights and flashes of nightmares that I could tell Noah felt too. An eternity past midnight, Jace finally pulled over at a small motel that looked like it had never seen a better day. Murmuring something about confirming if they'd take cash, he left the engine running and headed inside.

Maia nudged Dhanya, waking her up. Jace came back, nodding tiredly in lieu of giving us a more lengthy verdict. Maia handed him several bills without a word. A few minutes later found us in a tiny room with brown blankets and cheap artwork of random objects I was too sleepy to identify. Exhausted, I collapsed onto one of the beds.

The nightmares chased me, plaguing me with visions of flame and death till I opened my eyes the next morning.

Pale sunrise peeked bashfully past the edge of the thick curtains. In the other bed, Maia and Dhanya were curled around each other, still sleeping. Wrapped in blankets on the floor near me, Jace was likewise asleep, breathing deeply and showing no sign of waking.

Noah sat by the door, his gaze on the gap between the curtains and the wall. He glanced over when I spotted him, saying nothing.

I pushed the blankets away. I only vaguely remembered climbing beneath them, and they felt heavy and too warm now. Slipping my feet into my shoes, I crossed the cheap, stained carpet and sank down onto the linoleum by the entryway.

"Bad dreams?" Noah asked quietly.

Discomfort made me fidget. "Hard couple of days."

I could feel his agreement.

"Are you doing alright?" I asked him. "This far inland, I mean?"

A moment passed before he nodded. "I'll be fine."

Silence fell between us. I picked at a stray bit of dust on my jeans. "About what I did at the truck stop in Toledo… I'm sorry. I didn't mean to upset you."

He paused. The weirdest sensation came from him, like pain he was determined not to feel.

"Not your fault," he said.

My brow furrowed.

"I freaked," he admitted softly. "It took me by surprise, just…"

He went quiet.

"What?" I asked.

"Feeling human."

My chest hurt at the words. At the pain behind them. I reached out toward him.

He pulled away. "Don't. Please. I—"

"Why not?"

"Because it won't last. And because it's not me. Ari, I can't use you to feel like a real person. If I figure it out on my own, great. But if not…"

"Maybe this'll help you figure it out."

"Or maybe I'll hurt you. Maybe anything. I don't know."

He frowned, looking away.

I dropped my gaze to my lap. I wasn't sure how to tell him that I'd felt better after sharing magic with him too. That, whatever was happening to me, something about it seemed more *right* after that. I got the impression he wouldn't trust it, even if he'd know I was telling him the truth. The strange, churning feeling was back again. The one I couldn't make sense of.

"Thank you, though," he acknowledged quietly.

I glanced to him. My lip rose in a small smile.

He shifted position against the wall. "You're still doing okay too, yeah? After what happened yesterday?"

"I think so." I paused. "What *did* you do?"

He shrugged. "I can absorb magic. I can make it a part of myself, so I figured maybe I could help her."

"So now you're part enforcer."

I waited, hoping the words really were the joke I'd intended them to be.

Amusement flickered through his green eyes. "No. The magic is there, but it's not strong enough to do anything to me. Not unless I want it to, which I don't. It'll fade in a day or two."

I hesitated. "It won't hurt you, though?"

"No."

I nodded in response, relieved.

On the floor by the bed, Jace drew a deep breath and rolled

over, his eyes finding us on the far side of the room. He pushed up onto one elbow and ran a hand through his hair, turning the tousled mess into a slightly differently shaped one. "Everything alright?"

I could hear the guarded note in his voice. I suspected he trusted Noah more now than he had, but that didn't change everything.

He was still my protective older brother.

"Yeah," I said. "Ready to go soon?"

He nodded. Scrubbing a hand over his face to wake himself up, he sighed and then shoved the blankets away. In the other bed, Dhanya moved to sit up. Catching sight of us, she turned and nudged Maia, who groaned tiredly.

I climbed back to my feet and moved aside to give Noah the space to do the same. Dhanya and Maia had brought bags with clothes for themselves and me, though they hadn't been able to get anything for Jace. They hadn't wanted to rouse anyone's suspicions, and I was close enough to Maia's size that her clothes would work of me. Accepting the bundle from her, I gave Jace an apologetic look and then retreated to the bathroom.

Fifteen minutes passed and then we were all ready to leave. With barely a backward glance to the rundown motel, we piled into the SUV. A fast food place yielded up breakfast, and in no time we were back on the highway.

Miles swept by with flat plains and enormous sky and delivered us finally to mountains that swallowed the light and made me feel entirely too small. Weird nausea gnawed at me, leaving me feeling weak and growing worse as the hours passed, and it wasn't until I glanced to the front and saw Noah shivering that I realized it was coming from him.

I stopped myself from reaching out to him. With how I felt, I wasn't sure it would help.

The clock ticked on, inching toward late afternoon when we finally pulled into the mountain town of Fort Pedrosa, Colorado. At Noah's quiet directions, Jace steered the SUV past the tourist shops and onto a residential street. Pine trees towered over the houses, while behind us, the hilly road blocked the view of the main street. We continued along till a white bungalow appeared and Noah told Jace to stop.

Nervous tension rolled through Noah. He didn't take his eyes from the house while he pushed open the door.

I climbed out and followed him. A screen door allowed access to the enclosed porch, but Noah simply knocked on it, making no move to go past.

Seconds slid by. The main door opened.

Surprise flickered from him, breaking through his tension.

"Can I help you?" the old woman asked, hobbling toward us with the help of a polished wood cane.

"I'm looking for Olivia," Noah said.

Confusion clouded the woman's wrinkled face. "Olivia? Oh! You mean the nice young lady who sold us the house. She moved, dear."

"Do you know where?"

Her pale lips pursed thoughtfully. "Hmm, oh yes. Santa Lucina, California."

Shock radiated from Noah. "Ah. Okay. Thank you."

She smiled and returned to her house. He retreated down the steps.

I followed, confused. He seemed like someone had just punched him in the stomach. "Noah?"

He stopped.

"What is it?" I pressed, coming up beside him.

He hesitated. His gaze flicked toward me. My brow rose questioningly.

"Santa Lucina is where I used to live."

Without another word, he walked back toward the SUV, leaving me to follow.

Jace was standing by the driver's door. "Not here?"

Noah shook his head.

Jace glanced to me when nothing else came.

"We need to keep going," I said, watching Noah while he climbed back into the passenger seat.

"Where?"

I tugged open the door. "California."

# 12

## NOAH

I should have figured Olivia would move. I would have called to check before coming here, provided I'd had her number. But it made sense, now that the ocean wasn't painful to landwalkers anymore. A researcher like Olivia would have jumped at the chance to live where she could find a whole new field of study.

But Santa Lucina. Out of the whole coast, *why* Santa Lucina?

I grimaced. That probably made sense too. If there was anywhere Chloe and the other dehaians would be likely to come back to, it was that town.

But still…

Still nothing. I didn't want to go. I didn't want to bring this mess within a thousand miles of my family. Judges and enforcers and ruanir. I didn't want the people I loved anywhere *near* those things. I'd hoped that this would bring an end to it. That I could come to Fort Pedrosa and Olivia would work some kind of miracle to undo this.

Or something.

Discomfort made me shift position on the seat. My thoughts

flicked toward Ari, picking up her confusion and concern. I tried to ignore them. This would be over soon. It *needed* to be over soon, even if it meant going to Santa Lucina. Even if it meant seeing Baylie in order to find out where Olivia lived. I'd handle it.

And I'd make it there fine.

A shiver ran through me. I hadn't lied to Ari. I *would* be fine. This was harder than traveling as the Beast had ever been, mostly because it was slow as hell by comparison and therefore meant I spent longer without the stronger magic on the coasts pouring into me. And the dehaians hadn't ventured this far inland in great numbers yet, meaning that the magical exchange of energy they created by going between land and sea—the magical exchange that was what I actually *survived* on—wasn't much in attendance here either.

But it wasn't important. The minute we crossed the mountains and headed toward the ocean, it wouldn't be as hard to hold myself in human form.

Though my skin was looking rather gray.

I frowned, concentrating. A hint of color returned. I drew a breath for good measure.

The shakiness grew worse. I quit breathing, giving up the charade. I needed to save my energy.

"So, um," Ari began. "How far is it to Santa Lucina?"

"Too far for one day's drive," Jace said. "Why? You doing okay?"

"Fine. I just wondered."

Her answer was too fast. Jace glanced to her reflection in the rearview mirror. "Do we need to stop?"

"Jace," she insisted, "it's fine."

His mouth tightened.

Seconds slid past. I closed my eyes.

My awareness flickered with ghostly images of everything around me. I scowled, fighting to stay in human form.

"Noah?" Ari asked.

With effort, I looked back at her.

"What was your favorite food?"

My brow furrowed. She seemed almost desperate beneath the question. "What?"

"Your favorite food. When you were—oh." Ari glanced to the others. "Um, Noah used to be a greliaran before he became the Beast last year."

I could see their confusion.

Ari ignored it, turning to me again. "Food?"

I struggled to think and after a moment, the memory came back. "Calzones."

"Yeah? What kind?"

I stared at her.

Ari's eyebrows rose.

"Sausage and red pepper."

She nodded encouragingly. "Tell me something else about it. About being human."

I realized what she was trying to do. Reluctance hit me, only to be met by another wave of desperation from her.

"You tell me," I countered. "What do you like?"

A smile flickered across her face. "Grilled chicken and garlic mashed potatoes. You ever had those?"

I nodded.

"You remember what they taste like?"

I let myself focus on the memory. The smell and the texture and everything else I could think of. "Yeah."

"What about desserts?"

"Hot fudge sundaes."

"Oh, I love those. Remember how the chocolate feels in your mouth?"

I nodded again. It was helping. Crazy or not, it was helping. I wasn't breathing and my skin wasn't exactly healthy-looking, but the shakiness wasn't so bad anymore. Somehow, not thinking about *looking* human, but just remembering *being* it was making it easier to keep from losing control.

Funny how that was what I'd been avoiding all this time.

Ari's smile widened. She'd felt my surprise, and from the look of it, the fact this was working too.

"Did you ever try bubble tea?" she asked.

"Yeah."

"What was your favorite kind?"

She kept the questions coming, bringing up every food she could remember. After a while, Maia and Dhanya joined in and, gradually, the shakiness faded. Soon I was able to pretend breathing as well. By the time we rolled into a motel, I felt more stable than I had in ages.

"Thank you," I told Ari quietly while we walked to the motel room door.

She smiled. "It'll get better closer to the coast."

I nodded and then paused, curious at her tone when she'd said that. It wasn't a question. More like a statement that was true for her too.

She continued ahead of me into the room, not seeming to notice my reaction.

As with the previous night, the others took the beds while I sank down by the door. I could tell that Maia and Dhanya still thought it was strange that I didn't sleep, though Jace seemed to have gotten over it. I figured being helpful was better than pretending, though, especially when there weren't enough beds anyway. While the others drifted off, I watched the parking lot through a gap in the curtains, wary of anyone who looked like they might be coming toward our door.

Dull fear throbbed from Ari. I closed my eyes. And then there was that. Her nightmares were like a buzzing drill in the back of my mind. I didn't know what to do to stop them, or even if they had anything to do with me at all.

But they were exhausting.

Short bursts of panic spiked through her fear. My brow furrowed tightly. I'd tried waking her when we'd spent the night outside the truck stop, though I didn't think she remembered. She'd barely opened her eyes and when she'd drifted off to sleep again, the nightmares had returned as if I'd never woken her at all. I couldn't ask her *not* to sleep, which meant I was essentially stuck.

I propped my elbows on my knees and leaned my head against the wall, surrendering to another anxiety-filled night.

The dull droning of fear finally broke off when the sun crept over the horizon, and I looked over to find her grimacing while she pushed away from the bed. Her golden-brown hair was tangled and her gray eyes were red from lack of rest. A tired breath left her and then she caught sight of me.

I couldn't tell what she saw, but her grimace deepened.

On the floor, Jace rolled over and then paused to find her awake. "Again?" he asked Ari. "Since when are you a morning person?"

Pushing aside the blankets, she didn't respond.

The others got up. A few minutes later, we left the motel behind. Like yesterday, they bought breakfast at a fast food place and then continued onto the highway, though everyone looked considerably less enthused about the process than the day before.

We drove on. The interstate twisted through the desert, and gradually, all remainders of shakiness faded from me. Traces of the ocean permeated the air, though I suspected even a bloodhound would have trouble picking the scent of salt from the breeze. But magic thrummed through me nevertheless, and when we rolled toward the mountain range between us and Santa Lucina, I couldn't help but feel relief.

For that at least.

I pushed the thought aside. I needed to see Baylie, no matter how uncomfortable it made me. She was my only link to finding Olivia and getting this dealt with.

Time slid by. Santa Lucina came into view.

I had no idea what to say to my stepsister. Or really, what I should even call her now. The title had been accurate back when

I was a greliaran. Her dad had married my mom when Baylie and I were both little kids. We'd basically grown up together, despite the fact that she'd lived with my mom in Kansas and I'd lived with my dad in California. But we'd been close in our own way.

Until this.

Nervousness twisted through me. I couldn't drag my eyes from the town coming toward us. I felt Baylie in it—just a tinge of blue glow in my mind, but there.

I wished we were driving anywhere else.

"Where to?"

I blinked, turning to Jace. "What?"

"Where do we go?"

"Um, right. Just drive. I'll tell you where to turn."

He gave me a curious look, but he kept going. A wary sort of questioning came from Ari. I didn't move, waiting and hoping she wouldn't ask.

She didn't say a word.

The blue glow in my head became stronger. I focused on it, wondering while I did if Baylie would feel this. The sense of her location narrowed, though, and as we continued into town, I gave Jace directions on where to go.

At a street alongside the coast, I told him to slow down. A park waited to our left, the green grass running headlong into the sand and the ocean. A four-story apartment building with a red tile roof and wide patios faced the sea from the opposite side of the road. Sunlight shone on its white walls beneath the bright blue sky.

"There," I said.

He pulled over.

Baylie was on the top floor. I couldn't tell if she knew I was here yet.

"So, uh…" Ari began. "Who are we seeing here?"

I looked back at her. She'd picked up on my anxiety. I'd probably been giving her a headache with it. "My stepsister. She should know where we can find the landwalkers."

Understanding spread through her. Ari's gaze darted over the others. "We can stay in the car?" she offered to me.

I hesitated. I wanted to agree, but it felt childish. I had to deal with this. It was my own fault this was awkward. I should have gone back to see Baylie before now. I shouldn't have avoided everyone.

And Ari would feel everything anyway.

"It's alright," I said.

She eyed me, weighing the response, and then nodded.

We climbed from the SUV. The ocean rushed onto the sand in the distance, the sound nearly drowned beneath the noise of traffic passing us on the road. Sunlight beat down, brilliant in a way it never was farther inland. In silence, we started toward the apartment building while Jace fed quarters into the meter and then followed us.

I felt like flying apart from nervous energy alone.

A man pushed past the door just when we reached it and I caught the metal handle before the door swung closed, grateful at least for not needing to call upstairs to get inside. Ari held the door for the others while I headed in. Shadows surrounded me and the sounds of our footsteps echoed from the walls. Without a word to the others, I continued up through the building till I reached Baylie's floor.

She *had* to be able to tell I was here. Any second now, she'd come out into the hall.

Behind me, Ari murmured for the others to give me space. I didn't look back. By the dark wood of Baylie's door, I lifted a hand and knocked.

Seconds crawled by.

The door crept open.

She'd known.

Her blue eyes wide, she stared at me. Her hand covered her mouth as if holding something in.

"Noah?" Baylie whispered.

"Hey."

A shaky breath left her chest. Her gaze skipped over me like she couldn't believe what she saw. "You're…"

She moved toward me. I drew her into a hug, concentrating as hard as I could on what it'd been like to have warmth in my skin.

It didn't work.

She pushed back from me in alarm. "You're cold. You—"

I started to let her go. "I know. I'm sorry, I can't—"

She hugged me again, cutting me off. "Oh shut up, I don't care."

An incredulous laugh bubbled up in me at the words. My arms tightened on her.

"Where have you been?" she asked into my shoulder. "Are

you alright?"

I wasn't sure what to say.

She seemed to catch sight of the others watching us from the end of the hall. She tensed. "Who are they?"

I kept an arm around her while I looked toward them. "They're why I'm here. Part of why," I amended when she glanced to me.

Baylie hesitated. "Okay…" Stepping away from me, she motioned toward her door. "Tell them to come in?"

She retreated into her apartment.

I looked to Ari and then nodded toward the doorway. Not waiting, I followed Baylie inside.

The apartment was beautiful. On the far wall, the open French doors to the patio gave a view of the ocean and let in copious amounts of fresh air and natural light. A couch and chairs upholstered in abstract patterns of pale green and blue were arranged around a coffee table in the center of the large living room. To my right was a kitchen decorated in similar colors, while I could see a bedroom in soft shades of white and blue through a door to my left. Baylie's keys and cell phone occupied a narrow table by the front door, with several textbooks stacked beside them.

Ari came in behind me. "Hi," she said.

Baylie still looked uncomfortable. "Hi," she replied. "I'm, um… I'm Noah's stepsister, Baylie."

"I'm Ari. This is my brother Jace, my cousin Maia, and her fiancée Dhanya."

Baylie nodded. "Nice to meet you." She glanced around

quickly. "Uh, have a seat. Can I get anyone something to drink?"

"Oh, we're fine, thanks," Ari said. "You two probably want to catch up, so if you don't mind, we'll just check out the view for a while? I don't think any of us have seen the Pacific before."

Gratitude flickered through me. Ari's lip twitched in a tiny smile when she felt it.

Baylie glanced between us. "Sure. Noah?"

She walked toward the bedroom.

Nodding to Ari briefly, I headed into the other room. Baylie shut the door behind me.

Silence followed. Still standing by the door, Baylie watched me, her fingers interlacing and fidgeting against one another.

"They seem nice," she offered.

I shrugged. "They're alright."

She looked away, biting her lip.

"So," I tried. "Chloe told me Dad set this up?"

"Yeah."

"It's nice."

She nodded.

A moment slid by. I could hear the others talking in the next room, their words muffled by the door. Outside, a car honked in the distance. A bird landed on the flower box on the window.

"It, uh, it was a graduation present," Baylie said as if attempting to fill the quiet. "I tried staying back in Reidsburg, but it just..." She grimaced and then struggled to regroup. "I'm taking classes at Santa Lucina State this fall and I like it better out here anyway. Chloe and Zeke have the apartment across the hall for when they stay in town too, so it's… you know, it's alright."

I hesitated, not sure what to say. "Congratulations on graduating."

Baylie smiled. It looked strained. "Thanks. It was good. Chloe actually came back to finish out senior year, so I didn't have to be—"

I looked away.

"Have to be the only one," she finished in a rush. "I'm sorry. God, I'm sorry."

She came over, taking my hands. I pulled back, hating how cold I must feel to her. She tightened her grip, refusing to let go.

"It's okay," I said. "I get it."

"No, please, Noah. I am. I wasn't trying to make you feel bad."

"It's okay," I repeated. "I know you weren't. I just… I should have come to see you sooner."

Baylie hesitated. "Why didn't you?"

I shrugged again, unable to find the words to explain.

She was quiet for a moment. "So even greliaran-Beast hybrids get scared, huh?"

I blinked, looking back at her. Baylie's lips rose in a hopeful smile.

A small laugh escaped me. "Yeah, I guess."

Her smile grew.

I shook my head. "Damn, I missed you."

"Then don't stay away so long next time, eh?"

"Do my best."

She sank onto the edge of the white bedspread. I sat down next to her.

"Have you been to see your dad and Diane yet?" she asked.

I shook my head again, the humor fading. "They okay?"

She nodded. "Yeah. I mean, they miss you, but… yeah."

I echoed the motion. Silence returned.

"So who are they?" she asked, twitching her chin toward the door.

I searched for a response.

"Noah?"

"Have you talked to Zeke and Chloe this week?"

She paused. "They were here. Zeke had to head back for some kind of diplomatic thing yesterday and Chloe went with him. They just came because you said something was wrong with me. From the sound of it, you scared Chloe pretty badly. She wanted to leave soldiers here."

I winced. Of course I'd frightened Chloe, saying her best friend's name and then taking off like that.

"You *were* here the other day though, right?" Baylie continued. "I thought I, you know, *felt* you or…"

I nodded. "I'm sorry I couldn't stop."

"You— I mean I felt, like, pain. From you. Was that something to do with…" She twitched her head to the door again.

I hesitated. "Did Chloe say anything about wizards?"

Baylie blinked. "No."

I grimaced.

She glanced toward the other room. "They aren't…"

"They call themselves ruanir. And yeah, they are."

"But Joseph. They don't look like—"

"Same people, different survival strategy."

A breath left her.

"The girl, Ari. Their leaders connected her to me. Like you and Chloe, only *so* much stronger. That's what you felt. My reaction to them doing that to her."

Baylie stared at me. "It was horrible."

I nodded.

She looked to the door like she was processing what I'd said. I waited. It was weird. I could tell she was okay, if shaken, but other than that there was nothing.

After the flood of sensation from Ari over the past few days, it suddenly seemed odd to have such a faint connection to someone.

Baylie turned back to me. "So they're here now… why?"

"We're looking for Olivia. We need someone to help break this connection between us, and the elders are the best option we've got. None of Ari's people will help us and whenever I try… I can't. It's excruciating for her."

Even if I wasn't sure why and probably wouldn't ever find out.

I pushed the thought aside. I still didn't have an answer to whatever the Beast part of me had picked up on that night at the truck stop, but it didn't matter. We couldn't stay tangled up like this. We'd go crazy. Hell, I'd probably been causing Ari enough trouble between my struggle to stay looking like a human and to not freak out about seeing Baylie today.

"Well, um, Olivia's out of town," Baylie said. "Some land-walker thing. But Ellie's here."

"Ellie?" I repeated skeptically. "Baylie, we need someone who can use anything *approaching* magic. If Olivia's not around then I'll go to the dehaians. A landwalker elder just seemed like the fastest place to start."

Her lip twitched. "Don't underestimate the girl. She's incredibly good at what they can do, and she's been a provisional elder since last year. The other elders are going to make the status official soon."

My brow climbed.

Baylie grinned. "Come on. She's staying with her mom at Olivia's house for the summer. I'll call her and let her know we're on our way."

She rose to her feet.

I moved to do the same and then paused. "Baylie."

She looked back.

"I haven't told them about you. About the connection between us, I mean. They only know about my one with Chloe."

She hesitated, tension creeping back into her posture. "And you don't trust them," she said, only partly asking.

"I just want to keep you out of it. The bastards that are after Ari—after me—they nearly killed her brother and her cousin. They—" I grimaced. "I don't even *know* all of what they did to Ari, but they want to use that connection between us. They're willing to hurt her in order to hurt me."

Baylie was pale.

"I'm not saying we can't trust Ari and the others. I'm only trying to keep you as safe as I can."

She nodded tightly. Her brow flickering down, she turned back to the door, and a heartbeat went by before she pulled it open again.

I closed my eyes briefly and then followed her, hoping nothing came of what Ari and her family didn't know.

# 13

## ARI

The ocean breeze twisted in through the open French doors, stirring my hair and the flowers in the tall planters outside. The sound of the traffic carried with it, quieter than Chicago and undercut by the white-noise rush of so much water only a short distance away. Standing by the doorway, I watched it all, my gaze lingering on the waves rolling in toward the shore and the way their surfaces glinted in the sunlight.

Ruanir avoided the ocean. Even at our most careful, we could feel the magic there, tempting us. So it was better to stay away. Judge Engle's party was the closest I'd ever come to it.

And now I could feel it stronger than ever.

I shivered. I didn't think Noah had noticed my discomfort. He was distracted by seeing his stepsister again, and understandably so. But magic permeated the air all around us. I could tell it made the others anxious.

None of them wanted to end up poisoned like me.

I hugged my arms to my middle. I didn't *feel* poisoned. I'd seen the aftermath of someone with ocean magic poisoning before. A ruanir girl, when I was young. She'd gotten careless. She'd spread the contagion to her family and a half dozen of her friends before the judges had been able to intervene, and all of the infected had ended up with their abilities damaged and their minds never the same. So I had to figure the fact that *wasn't* happening to me was part of what the judges had done.

At least, I hoped it wasn't happening to me.

I shivered harder.

But meanwhile, I was… I wasn't sure what. Better, maybe. Almost tingly with energy, like oxygen filled me again after too long without air. It was probably a reaction to Noah feeling stronger after what he'd been through while we traveled, but it was still disconcerting.

The breeze picked up. My arms pulled tighter against my stomach.

"Are you okay?"

I glanced over. Maia eyed me worriedly. Behind us, Jace and Dhanya were sitting on the couch, talking in low voices.

"Yeah," I said, nodding.

She looked like she wanted to put an arm around me, but was holding herself back from it.

"You?" I asked.

"Oh, yeah. Fine. Just…"

Her gaze didn't quite go to the view beyond the patio.

"Yeah," I agreed.

She bit her lip. "You're not in pain though, right? Dhanya said it hurt you when he helped me."

I hesitated. "I feel what he feels."

She seemed to search for words. "So like, just physical stuff, or…"

I shook my head. "All of it."

Her gaze darted to the bedroom door, questioning.

"He's been a nervous wreck the whole day," I said quietly. "It seems to be going well in there, though."

Maia paused, appearing taken back. "That has to be hard. On you, I mean. Having somebody in your head like that."

I watched a bicyclist speed past on the sidewalk. "Yeah. On him too."

A moment passed. A breath escaped her. "Weird to think about something like that… the *Beast*… being nervous."

I glanced to the door. I supposed it was.

And I supposed it was weird that I'd *stopped* thinking about it too. He was more person to me now than monster. Just a guy, worried about seeing his family again after so long.

It was so ordinary.

The bedroom door opened. Noah followed Baylie out. With a tight smile to us, she crossed the room to the console table and retrieved her cell phone. Carrying it with her, she headed back toward the bedroom and slipped past Noah.

Her door closed again.

Noah came over to me. "Olivia's out of town. Baylie's calling another elder we know."

I nodded. Maia gave him an uncomfortable smile and then retreated toward the others.

"So," I said to him quietly. "That…"

"Went good, yeah." He paused. "Sorry about today. If I was,

you know…"

He motioned abstractedly to his head.

"Payback for all the nightmares, right?" I joked.

His lip twitched.

"It's fine," I told him. "It wasn't that bad."

He nodded, seeming relieved.

The door opened again. Baylie came out.

"Ellie will be waiting for us," she said to Noah. "She'll see what she can do to help you."

"Alright." He glanced around. "So, um…"

"We can just meet you there?" Baylie offered, watching Noah with a hesitant expression. "If you want to, like…"

She twitched her head toward the outside.

He hesitated. "Car's better. Their leaders can track me the other way."

She blinked. "Oh. Okay. Then I guess, um, if you want to ride with me, they can follow?"

Noah glanced to me. We hadn't tried being that far apart since this happened. Not for long, anyway.

I didn't figure anything would go wrong.

My stomach twisted.

Noah seemed to feel the same. "Ari, you want to maybe—"

"Yeah." I looked to Jace. "Could you guys take the SUV and I'll ride with them?"

Jace opened his mouth as if to protest, but Maia cut in before he could speak. "Yeah, sure," she said. "We'll follow you."

I gave her a smile. We headed for the door.

Baylie's red car waited in a parking garage in the basement

of the building. I took the back seat, leaving Noah up front with her. She pulled out onto the street and then steered the car deeper into town.

Silence hung heavy. I wasn't sure what to do to break it, or even if I should. I could see her glancing at us both from the corner of her eye, me in the rearview mirror and Noah beside her. For his part, he seemed anxious again, but with that weird, churning energy back as well.

The combination was confusing to say the least.

On a narrow street that traced a line across the hillside, Baylie pulled over. A two-story bungalow with pale gray siding and white accents waited just beyond the sidewalk next to us. An African-American girl with curling braids sat on the porch steps, intently studying something on the tablet computer in her hand.

Noah pushed open the door. I climbed out as well, while the SUV came to a stop behind us.

The girl looked up. A smile spread over her face, tinged with a shyness I could see from the car. She set the tablet on the step and then rose to her feet.

"Hey Ellie," Baylie called as we walked toward her. "Thanks for agreeing to help."

I tried to hide my surprise. *This* was Ellie? The girl looked barely sixteen. Surely she wasn't a landwalker elder?

Ellie nodded. "Oh, yeah. Of course." Her unusual, tan-green eyes turned toward Noah. "Hi."

"Hey," he replied.

She hesitated as if she wanted to say something more, but

then her eyes darted over me and the others. She smiled shyly instead and retreated toward the house.

I looked to Noah. "She's...?"

Baylie seemed to hear my skepticism. "*She* singlehandedly took on a greliaran bigger than him." She twitched her head toward Noah. "And she won."

I blinked. Surprise radiated from Noah as well.

Baylie gave Noah a pointed glance. "Told you not to underestimate her."

She grinned and headed inside. Without a word, we followed.

The interior of the house was airy and cool, owing to open windows on either side of the long living room to the left of the entryway. A staircase on my right led to the upper floor, while directly ahead, the hall ended in a brightly decorated kitchen.

"Just have a seat anywhere," Ellie said, gathering papers and books from the sofas occupying the living room. "Sorry it's such a mess. Mom and I are researching some old magic stuff for Olivia. I was going to clean while Mom's at the store, but I got caught up."

"Don't worry about it," Baylie assured her.

Jace came through the door behind me, Maia and Dhanya on his heels. He paused, watching Ellie. "So this is the—"

"Yeah," I said.

Jace's eyebrows rose. We walked into the living room while Ellie hurried out, a bundle of papers in her arms. Four large couches circled the coffee table in the center of the space, while the area at the end of the room that had been obviously designed for a dinner table held a large computer desk and several monitors instead.

We sank onto the couches, Noah taking a seat at the opposite end of the leather sofa from me and everyone else finding places on the other three couches surrounding the coffee table. A cool breeze carried in the noise of kids playing somewhere in the neighborhood, the sound thin and strange over the distance.

"So," Ellie said when she came back into the room. "I just had a couple questions first, if you don't mind?"

Sitting down on the brown suede couch across from me, she waited for my answer.

I shrugged. "Sure."

Ellie smiled anxiously. "Great. Thank you. So Baylie tells me you're, um…"

"Wizards," Baylie offered quietly.

Ellie didn't take her eyes from us.

I glanced to the others and then gave a small nod. "Yeah."

"We prefer the term ruanir," Jace added.

"Okay…" Ellie allowed. "So how come we don't know about you? I mean, you know about us, right? Landwalkers?"

I looked to Jace. This was awkward. "Yeah, we do. We just—"

"Alright, but we have—" Ellie motioned to the computers. "We do a *lot* of research. We have connections everywhere. Police, government. If there were people doing magic, *someone* would have noticed. So how is it you stayed hidden?"

I searched for an answer.

"Money," Maia said quietly.

Ellie looked to her.

"Money is magic too."

Ellie blinked.

"Most of our people are rich," Jace filled in. "We…" A breath left him. I could see him debating about what to say.

"Just tell them," I said.

He watched me for a moment and I could just see the thoughts running through his mind. They were the same ones any ruanir always had. We grew up on secrecy. It was the key to our survival. Even this was saying too much. And the judges would take action against anyone who told.

But then, they'd already tried to kill us. What more could they do?

And Noah would know if I heard anyone lie.

"Jace," I said.

He grimaced. "If you have enough money," he continued reluctantly, "you can stay out of sight. You don't have to work, you can buy isolated houses, new identities if you want them… anything. Many of our families are millionaires, if not billionaires, and those who aren't get help from our leaders, the Judiciary, to move around too." He sighed. "It's not really in our best interest to be noticeable. Humans aren't great at putting up with things that are different, and if they turned on us… Our magic is slow. Even with extra power stored in jewelry or whatever, the energy still takes time to build up before we can use it. We wouldn't last five seconds against guns or bombs or whatever, and none of us want to end up in a lab.

Add to that the Judiciary, who punishes any unauthorized, external use of magic—as opposed to the internal use of just sharing it between ourselves—and you've got a pretty decent system for staying hidden."

"But where does the money *come* from?" Ellie pressed.

Jace's gaze flicked back to me briefly, his jaw working around. "Us, mostly. We leave inheritances, we have investments, we've built fortunes over centuries. And we can do that because…"

"Because we don't really age," Maia supplied when he trailed off. "Not like humans."

I didn't take my eyes from my cousin, but I could feel the others staring at us.

"We call it the adjustment," she explained. "It happens when we're about eighteen or so—human years. Jace just went through it. He started a bit later than normal. Dhanya and I did about a year ago. Ari will soon. It comes from an accumulation of specific kinds of magic and how they interact with your body after you reach a certain age. Our ancestors figured out how to use land magic to change themselves in an effort to hide from—" She nodded her head toward Noah. "—and since we're born basically human and magic is something we learn through exposure, the Beast never finds us as children. So we grow up, our parents expose us to this magic, and then eventually we use it ourselves. Then, when we're old enough and our bodies are ready for it…" She shrugged. "We adjust. And gradually we start growing older more slowly."

"How slowly?" Ellie asked.

"We figure the average is about one year to every four

human ones. Something close to that. Gets even slower as time passes, though."

Baylie let out a short breath, looking speechless. But worse was Noah. His shock was overwhelming.

"So yeah," Maia continued. "We leave money to ourselves, more or less. To alternate identities or whatever. We shuffle accounts around, keep an eye out for new things to invest in that look promising.  Some of our people continue working, others take a decade or so off, and the ruanir who don't have as much money for one reason or another get help from the Judiciary."

She sighed. "The judges *do* have connections inside the government and the police or whatever. They're the only ones, though. Anyone else who tries to manipulate the human world…" Maia glanced to Dhanya and Jace, her mouth thinning briefly. "They're seen as possibly risking the exposure of the ruanir. So the Judiciary controls that. But they're also not very hands-on, which is probably why you've never heard of us. Their influence is mostly through human proxies—lobbyists and various others the judges hire. Anything more would risk drawing too much attention when the judges didn't age over time, so in that respect, the judges stay below the radar like the rest of us." She shrugged. "If you have enough money and you're careful about it, you can do that."

Silence followed for a moment. I fought the urge to fidget uncomfortably on the couch.

"So how old are you?" Baylie asked, her voice careful like she thought we might bite.

"We're how old we look," Maia replied. "It was only a year ago for Dhanya and me so we're… what would you say?"

She glanced to Dhanya.

"Maybe a month slowed down by this point?" Dhanya offered. "Possibly less than that."

"But the others…" Baylie pressed.

"My mom's maybe a hundred and fifty in human years," I said. "She stopped counting a long time ago."

"Right about the point she turned thirty in human years," Jace supplied dryly.

I tried to smile. It was hard. The shock coming from Noah had changed into a bizarre tension and wariness, like he suddenly didn't know how to be around me and wanted to leave. It was upsetting. I wasn't a freak, not any more than a cold-skinned guy who could turn into a thunderstorm. We were just different than humans. I thought he'd already figured that out.

And meanwhile, the room had gone quiet. In the distance, the kids were still playing. The sound only made the silence around me more uncomfortable.

"Okay, well," Ellie tried tentatively. "Thank you for answering my questions. I guess we should get started, then."

I looked over at her, grateful for the lifeline even if what she said made my stomach twist. "What are you going to do?"

She bit her lip briefly. "You know about landwalkers. What do you know about the elders?"

"Just that you're in charge of the others like you," I allowed.

Not that she looked old enough for anyone to listen to her.

"Oh." Ellie blinked. "Um, well, not really. We do keep the

history and help our people with problems and stuff, but that's not exactly what I meant. Do you know about what we can do?"

I shook my head slowly. "I guess not."

She nodded. "Right. So, basically, we can make people be the same as us. Like, um…"

Ellie glanced to Baylie and Noah as if seeking help.

"Like," Baylie filled in, "if she locks onto you and then closes her eyes, you won't be able to see either."

I blinked. "I-I didn't know landwalkers could do that."

Ellie seemed embarrassed. "It's just a mental trick the elders have. But sometimes we can make it go a different way. Sort of the reverse, though it's more difficult. Not all of us can do that part. But turns out I can, and that'll let me feel what it's like to *be* you. Maybe see if I can get a handle on what this connection is at the same time."

I stared at her and from the corner of my eye, I could see the others doing the same. "So… then what happens?" I asked into the silence.

"Well…" Ellie shrugged. "Then I see if I can break your connection to Noah without hurting either of you. Worst case, I'll have a feel for it so then we can talk to the dehaian doctors and find out if *they* know what to do. They're the ones with more experience in ocean magic anyway, and since that's sort of what he *is*—" Her gaze twitched to Noah. "—that's probably the next step."

"You talk with dehaian doctors?" Noah asked.

"Some." Ellie nodded. "We're still trying to figure out how

to get landwalkers to change form like the dehaians can, and lots of the dehaian doctors are just as curious about it as we are, so…"

She shrugged again.

Anxiety fluttered in me. "What do we need to do?"

"Well…" Ellie took a deep breath. "If you could just stay where you are, we can try it now."

"Just like…?"

Ellie smiled. "Right there. And don't worry, I've done this a bunch of times before. I promise it won't hurt."

My gaze darted to Jace. Our people had always thought the landwalkers and their elders were just humans with a weird ancestry—a group to be avoided or, in crueler circles, something of a joke.

We'd been wrong.

They were vaguely terrifying.

"Ready?" Ellie asked.

"I-I guess, if you—"

My world spun. I was in my own head and looking at myself from across the room at the same time. I could feel the suede couch and the leather one. Sound came from too many directions, echoing inside my ears. I closed my eyes, gasping.

The sensations vanished and then it was just me. But not me. There were two of me in my head, like a sound and echo but so similar, I couldn't be sure which one was real. The echo hovered, filling the same space as the sound like two realities laid impossibly on top of the other.

And beneath them both, a quivering shook the darkness.

I wondered at it. Wondered at what I was perceiving inside my own mind like I'd never been here before.

And then I fell deeper. But I didn't. My other self sank by me. Through me, like I was a connecting hall between two rooms.

Fear flickered inside me, not echoed, not mirrored. This wasn't right. I shouldn't… *she* shouldn't go there… she shouldn't…

The fear spiked higher. The quivering grew stronger. Violent. My other self rushed past me, out of me like the hounds of hell were on her tail. And something was wrong. The whole world was shaking. I wasn't—

Lightning exploded in my mind.

I tried to scream.

And blinding oblivion swallowed me.

Children played, their laughter ghostly.

Someone swung me up and tossed me high into the air, only to catch me.

Ocean water rushed around my bare feet, its passage stinging over the tiny scrapes left on my skin after the car accident I'd caused.

"Ari…"

I opened my eyes.

Noah was above me. His hand was pressed to my cheek and magic rushed into me through the contact. His deep green eyes searched mine. "Are you okay?"

A ragged breath entered my lungs. I was on something hard. The ceiling looked too far away. Jace stood behind Noah, worry on his face.

Memory started to return. "Ellie."

Noah looked to the side. I pulled my gaze over.

I lay on the floor. The coffee table had been shoved out of the way, leaving open space around me. Maia and Dhanya were standing near it, their eyes on me, and Dhanya had her cell phone in her hand like she'd been in the middle of dialing a number. On the opposite couch, Ellie sat, breathing hard and trembling. Baylie was next to her, but they both were watching me.

"What happened?" I asked.

Noah hesitated. "You had some kind of a seizure."

I looked back to him, alarmed. His face tightened at the feeling.

"Are you alright?" Dhanya asked, tucking her phone away.

"Yeah, I… I think so."

I tried to sit up. Noah moved to help me. "Careful," he urged.

Nodding, I shuffled around till my back pressed to the side of the couch and my hand braced me on the floor. Noah stayed by my side. Apprehension coming off of him in waves, he took my free hand, watching me.

His skin was like ice. He was pouring whatever he had into me.

My breath caught and I looked over at him.

"I'm okay," he said, reading something in my expression.

I started breathing again. I couldn't quite let go of the worry this was hurting him—even if here by the ocean, he probably was right about being okay—but I nodded.

"What the hell did you do?" Jace demanded of Ellie.

"Hey!" Baylie snapped. "Back off. This wasn't her fault."

Jace glowered, his gaze going from Ellie to Baylie, and then he turned away.

Ellie shivered. "I-I didn't know she'd react like this. I swear. It should've been fine."

"What *did* happen?" Dhanya asked.

Ellie looked to me as if waiting for the answer.

I hesitated. The memories were foggy. Some of them didn't make sense. I'd never been in ocean water, never been in a car accident let alone caused one. "I don't know."

"Me… I think."

I turned to Noah, confused.

He grimaced. "I could feel that. What Ellie did and…" He shook his head, humiliation radiating from him. "I don't know, really. That thing landwalker elders do, it must have some similarity to how the dehaians were able to make me. The Beast. Whatever." His jaw worked around. "Ellie, I am *so* sorry. It didn't even occur to me that—"

"No," she apologized quickly. "I should've thought of it too. If you felt that through your connection to her and it was anything like what they did, then of *course* it would make that part of you—"

"What? Try to kill you over some centuries-old PTSD?"

Contempt for himself was thick in Noah's voice. He looked like he wanted to leave the room.

My hand tightened on his. He didn't quite glance my direction.

But he didn't move away either.

I swallowed hard. He was right—about the fact it'd come from him, anyway, though definitely *not* about how he should have known that his plan for helping us both would result in this. But a split second before everything had gone black, I'd felt a surge of protectiveness and rage rush at me, like some incredible force had been trying to obliterate a danger it perceived. And not just a danger to itself.

To me.

I shifted position against the couch. I was okay, though. The magic coming from Noah was helping. I still felt shaky, but it wasn't as bad. And I knew I should let him go. This had to be draining him, no matter what he said. But I didn't want to. His hand felt good. Cold, yes. But grounding, like even that tiny contact was tethering me back from the horrible blur of light and sound of the seizure.

"Can we get you something?" Dhanya tried after a moment. "A glass of water or…?"

My stomach churned hard at the thought. "No, thanks."

Noah glanced to me. I could feel his confusion at my reaction.

I didn't meet his gaze. So I didn't want a drink. It wasn't *that* strange. I still felt too shaky for anything.

He turned back to Ellie. "So what did you find out?

Anything?"

Ellie fidgeted on the couch. "Well, obviously it's strong. This connection, it's not like—"

She hesitated, catching sight of the nervousness that flashed across Baylie's face, even as tension spiked through Noah. My brow furrowed in confusion.

"N-not like anything I've ever seen," she continued awkwardly. "The magic in it is strange. But that's not the only problem."

Her gaze went to me, shy but certain. "I'm sorry."

I stared at her, my confusion growing. "What?"

"It's not just the connection. Whoever made this… they've done something to you. Changed you. I could feel what you *think* you are to yourself. Your sense of what and who you are. But beneath it, there's a dissonance. It's like something's shifting."

I couldn't breathe.

"Could it be the poisoning?" Maia asked faintly. "If that's starting to damage her…"

Ellie hesitated.

"What was it?" I pressed, my heart pounding. "My abilities? My mind? What's changing?"

Ellie looked worried. "Everything."

I trembled.

"I don't know what this 'poisoning' is," Ellie continued. "But what was done to you feels deliberate. Like someone put something new into you; twisted things around in a certain way. It's growing through you, all subtle so you wouldn't pick up on it. And it doesn't feel like his magic. I—" Her gaze darted to Noah. "I recognize that. This is something else. It's tangled up in that connection between you two, though." She shifted uncomfortably. "It's feeding on it."

I felt Noah go still. The magic coming from him stuttered to a halt. His hand inched from mine like he was afraid I'd break.

I couldn't take my eyes from her. "Do you know what it, um… what I'm…" The words wouldn't come.

Ellie shook her head. "No."

"What *could* you tell?" Noah asked, his voice tight.

"It's hard to say," Ellie said. "I don't know what the end result is supposed to be. But if you've only been connected for a few days…"

Her voice made the question clear. Noah nodded.

Ellie grimaced. "It's strong. In that short an amount of time, it's gotten *really* strong. I'm guessing it wouldn't have been too much longer before both of you realized something was wrong."

I was shaking so hard it hurt. Tears burned in my eyes, stupid and futile. They'd done this. The judges had done this. They'd lied and tricked me and…

Stage one. When I'd woken up, they'd said stage one.

"What can we do?" Noah asked.

I looked over at him. He was pulling back from me, from the connection between us, and it hurt. I knew he could feel how it hurt. But there was something else, a quivering and horrified shame, and it made me want to reach out to him.

This wasn't his fault. I'd let them do this to me. I'd believed them and trusted them because they led our people. I'd thought the Judiciary wanted the best for us.

And I'd been such a fool. Our world was so messed up. I'd just never realized it, not until it nearly killed us all.

"I'm not sure," Ellie answered him. "That magic… like I said, it's not like anything I've ever seen. I don't even know if the dehaians could—"

"The judges," Maia interrupted.

I turned to her, confused.

"It's the judges," she continued. "They're the ones who did this. So if the landwalkers or the dehaians can't help, then we have to make a judge fix this."

My brow furrowed. "Where are we going to—"

"Dad," she said.

Fear twisted through me. "Maia, we can't—"

"He's in Australia," Jace protested.

Maia shook her head. "Not anymore. Last week, the Judiciary called back nearly every judge they had overseas, including him. He's been reassigned near the town of Grayland, up on the Washington coast. He should be there in a few days."

I stared at her. It couldn't be a coincidence, all the judges returning here. Not after the dehaians' attack at Judge Engle's house.

My stomach quivered.

"He could help you," Maia said to me.

Noah made an incredulous sound. "Or he could make this worse! Those judge bastards set this all up. What makes you think he won't just turn us over to them?"

"We'll be careful," Maia insisted. "Dhanya, Jace, and I will go with Ari to see him. You stay out of sight. We tell him that we've gotten away from you because this is hurting Ari. That whatever the judges intended, it's gone wrong. We insist he break it because she's in trouble."

"And if he *doesn't*?"

"We say she's dying. Make it serious."

"Maia," Jace said. "This is *incredibly* dangerous. If he tries anything—"

"Noah stops him." She looked back to Noah. "This connection thing. It'll let you know if something's gone wrong, right?"

Shock and disbelief came from Noah. He seemed to struggle for a response. "Yeah."

Maia nodded like that settled it. "This is the best option. Maybe the only one. We have to stop this from hurting Ari."

I didn't know what to say. I never wanted to come near a judge again as long as I lived.

"Maia's right," Dhanya admitted, discomfort in her eyes. "There's no other choice."

Jace let out a breath, looking away. I shivered, wishing they were wrong and knowing they weren't.

"Alright," I said quietly.

Frustration radiated from Noah. "You can't be serious," he protested to me, a touch desperately. "If he tries to hurt you…" He looked to Maia. "Do you really want to risk what I might have to *do* to him to stop that? He's your *father*."

"He's a judge."

Maia's voice was hard. Almost cold, but for the tense note of pain and loss beneath it. Dhanya looked toward her sympathetically, while surprise came from Noah at her words.

But then, he didn't know what having a judge for a parent was like.

Jace pushed to his feet. "We'll head out tomorrow after we've all had a chance to rest."

I nodded tightly. Bracing myself on the floor, I started to rise. Noah tensed as if stopping himself from helping me.

Discomfort twisted through me. Noah had been the only one able to touch me in days. Somehow, the fact that the others couldn't come near me hadn't seemed so bad because of him. And now that was over. The others were all watching, their expressions making clear that Noah wasn't the only one who wanted to help. But none of them could. I'd hurt them or they'd hurt me, all because of the poison inside me and what the judges had done.

My legs wobbling unsteadily beneath me, I reached my feet, feeling suddenly very alone in the middle of a room of people. I knew Noah picked up on it. Whether or not he'd pulled away from the connection between us, a strange sort of discomfort was coming from him too.

We headed for the door. Dhanya murmured pleasantries as they left, her hand holding Maia's supportively. Ellie smiled, that same nervous look in her eyes that took on a tinge of apology when I came closer.

"I'm really sorry that I couldn't help," she said.

I nodded. "Thank you for trying."

Her anxious smile returned.

I walked toward the porch steps.

"See you later," I heard Baylie tell her behind me.

"Yeah," Ellie agreed.

Noah and Baylie followed me down the stairs. Up ahead, the lights flashed on Baylie's car when she pressed the key fob to unlock the door.

"Should Ari maybe, um…" Baylie started.

I glanced back.

"Maybe you should take the other car," she told me, her gaze twitching toward her stepbrother.

I hesitated.

"Yeah," Noah said, not looking at me.

A tiny breath left me. I dropped my gaze away. "Right."

"We'll meet you back at Baylie's," Noah called to the others.

Jace nodded and then climbed into the SUV.

My gaze crept toward Noah. He grimaced when he saw me look his way, guilt joining the tension inside him.

"Just don't let the cars get too far apart, alright?" he told Baylie. "Distance hurts."

Baylie hesitated. "Alright."

Noah nodded tightly. His gaze twitched back to me. "We'll fix this," he promised.

I nodded too, trying desperately to believe him. "Yeah."

Feeling more alone than ever, I headed for the SUV.

There wasn't much discussion of us finding a motel when we got back to Baylie's apartment. We were all low on cash after traveling across the country and Baylie didn't seem to want to send her stepbrother away after not seeing him for a year. As a group, we'd climbed up to the top floor, mostly silent but for our footsteps on the stairs.

And no one came close to me.

Dinner was pizza and nothing in particular followed, except for awkward attempts at conversation which died from no one having much to say. When darkness fell, it almost felt like a relief, the night giving us all an excuse to go to bed and forget this day till tomorrow. Baylie owned a large air mattress—something her dad and stepmother used when they came to visit from Kansas, she told us—and while Jace and Dhanya washed the dishes, Maia and Noah helped her retrieve it from the closet.

I took cushions from the chairs, setting up my own bed. Jace had spent every night in the motels on the ground and I'd had enough. He could have the couch while Maia and Dhanya had the air mattress. My brother needed decent rest too.

The silence was deafening after everyone fell asleep, though.

Lying on the cushions with a thin blanket over me, I stared at the white, scallop-textured drywall of the ceiling. I couldn't close my eyes. My thoughts bounced around like balls inside a pinball machine, erratically going nowhere with great velocity, only to tumble into nothing and start their cycle again. I wanted to know what had changed about me. What dissonance Ellie had detected. And at the same time I didn't, as if lying here repeating to myself how *normal* I felt would somehow prove that what she'd told me wasn't true. I couldn't be changing. Surely I would know.

My stomach twisted. I wondered what the judges planned for me to become.

On the air mattress, Maia rolled over. Dhanya shifted around, wrapping her arm around Maia again without ever seeming to wake up.

I closed my eyes. I'd be fine. They'd be fine. We'd all be fine and this would be over soon.

I wondered what nightmares would be waiting for me tonight.

The twisting in my stomach grew worse.

I pushed the blanket aside. My bare feet sank into the thick carpet and around me, no one else moved. Moonlight streamed in through the French doors, turning the room to shades of deep blue and silver. Picking my way past the others quickly, I crossed to the doors and eased one open.

Noah glanced up from his seat on the porch floor. His legs were drawn up, his elbows resting on his knees, and his back leaned on the wall of the apartment building. Tall planters overflowing with flowers surrounded the patio, shielding him from sight of the street below, though gaps between them afforded a narrow view of the sea.

"Can we talk?" I whispered.

He nodded.

Gratitude flickered through me. I slipped outside and then pulled the door closed behind me. The breeze tugged at my nightshirt and shorts, the air laden with salt and magic and making me shiver. I sank down onto the porch beside him.

The wood slats were cool beneath me and I wrapped my arms around my knees, hugging them close for warmth.

Beyond the beach across the street, waves tumbled against the shore, the black water barely visible in the darkness. My gaze lingered on it. I wondered how cold it was at this time of night.

"Good conversation," Noah commented after a few moments.

I blinked. A chagrinned chuckle escaped me. "Sorry."

He made a neutral sound.

I hesitated. "You doing alright?"

Skepticism came from him. That wasn't why I'd come out here and he knew it. "Yeah."

I didn't respond. A weird strain followed the word, almost like he was lying. My brow drew down.

"Really," he insisted to the silent question.

A heartbeat passed, then another.

His mouth tightened. "I was just thinking about what you said. Or, what Jace and Maia said. The 'adjustment' thing."

I looked away. His discomfort and shock had been obvious earlier. But it still seemed unjustified. He'd known we were different, and I didn't want to be interrogated about those differences right now.

I already had more of them—no, *possibly* had more of them; I was fine, really—than I could handle.

"What's it like?" he asked.

I turned back to him, surprised by the question.

His gaze was on the ocean like he could read something

from the waves.

I tried for a shrug. "I don't know. I haven't gone through the adjustment, so—"

"No, not…" He frowned.

"What?"

He was silent and for a moment, I wasn't certain he was going to continue.

"What's it like knowing you're going to outlive every single human you see?"

The words stole mine. My mouth moved while I searched for a response.

"I've lived for centuries, Ari," he said quietly. "I remember islands falling into the ocean so long ago, no one knows their names. And I would have turned eighteen this year. I have a family. Friends. I remember being a kid. I don't even know what I *am* anymore, but now…"

His gaze dropped away again.

"That why you didn't come back till today?" I asked softly.

He didn't take his eyes from the porch slats, something about his face seeming so old and so young at the same time. "Mostly."

I waited. He didn't say anything more.

I looked away. I wasn't certain what to tell him. We weren't like him. Our situation wasn't remotely the same. We lived for centuries too, but we had our friends and families with us.

We weren't the only one of our kind.

A shiver bubbled up, freezing me in place. That *we* sort of assumed I even went through the adjustment anymore. That what the judges were making me into hadn't taken that away. For all I knew, Noah and I might have the opposite problem.

I made myself take a breath. I couldn't think about that. I'd be fine. I *was* fine.

"We stay around people who understand us," I told him, my voice all the more firm for how I didn't want to dwell on anything else. "With people who know what that's like… even just a little bit."

He turned to me, his green eyes so dark, they appeared almost as black as the ocean.

I swallowed, strangely warm chills rippling through me, stealing my breath. Looking down, I struggled to still them.

Silence stretched between us. Waves crashed in the distance. My fingers picked at a small stone wedged between slats of the porch.

"You didn't come out here to talk about that," he said quietly.

My hand paused on the stone.

"You alright?" he continued.

"Yeah."

He didn't believe me. I turned my face away.

"I…" A breath left me. "I can't stop thinking about it. About how they—" I fidgeted. "I mean, I'm *fine*. I don't… I don't *feel* different. I'm just…"

My heart started pounding again, same as it had in the living room. I hugged my legs close, attempting to calm down. "What was it like, becoming the Beast?"

Noah paused. "You're not like me, Ari."

I looked over at him.

He grimaced faintly. "I could tell something was changing in you a few days ago. I just didn't know what it was—or what to say. But it doesn't feel like me. I thought for a while it might be, but—" He shook his head. "—whatever they've tried to do to you, it's not this."

I stared at him.

"I'm sorry I didn't tell you," he said.

My brow furrowed and I turned away, uncertain how to respond. My gaze slipped to the dark water again, something about it calming me despite the danger of the magic there.

"I wish I was," I murmured.

I felt his surprise.

My shoulder rose in a tiny shrug. "I guess, it…" I searched for the right words. "It doesn't seem like it'd be that bad, being like you." My gaze drifted across his hands and his arms and the shadows from the muscles there. "I mean, yeah, there're differences, and maybe some of it's hard. But you're still a person. You're still you. With what the judges can do to people, how they can just take away *everything*…"

His hand moved toward mine and then he caught himself.

A pained feeling pierced my chest, driven by the fear of what might happen if we didn't stop this. Of how I might never touch another person again.

How I might not even remember *wanting* to.

I reached out toward him.

Noah pulled away. "I don't want to hurt you."

I let out a ragged breath, desperate to explain how much I didn't care about that. How I could be careful. I knew accidentally absorbing magic from him had started all this, but right now, that almost didn't matter to me.

A twinge of regret flickered through him, as if in reaction to my thoughts. My eyes rose to his.

He was watching my hand. I couldn't be sure of what I was feeling from him. Discomfort, but strange.

"Please?" I whispered.

His hand moved toward me. His skin brushed mine, cold yet gentle. Our fingers tangled together. A hint of uncertainty flashed past the connection between us and my grip tightened on his. I didn't want him to let go.

Gingerly, he drew me closer. His hand broke from mine only long enough for his arm to slip around my shoulders.

A breath left me while he held me to his side. He was cool like the night around me and his chest was still where a heartbeat should have been, but I didn't care. The cold didn't matter. This was him. A person, still able to be near me. A guy who continued to be kind, even when he so easily could have hated me for everything I'd done.

"Thank you," I whispered.

He hesitated, something flickering through him so fast, I couldn't catch it before it was gone. "You're welcome."

I closed my eyes, resting my head on his shoulder. Waves tumbled in the distance, the sound carrying on the breeze.

My thoughts drifted. Flames twisted like ghosts in the darkness behind my eyes, growing brighter with every heartbeat. My brow furrowing, I tried to hold them at bay. I didn't want to have those nightmares again.

A cool sensation spread across me, like black water slipping over my skin. The rippling cold rose up to drown the flames and surround me, never once making me feel in danger at all. A feeling of vast power came from it, enough to shake the mountains, enough to tear the sky, yet peaceful in this moment like a murmur meant to calm. The fire and my fear melted away, soothed into nothing by the dark water caressing me.

I drew a breath, opening my eyes.

Light touched the sky beyond the patio, painting swaths of gold and salmon pink across the indigo. Birds chirped in the trees, unseen beyond the tall planters that mostly sheltered us from view. His arm around me, Noah was still in a way I'd never felt from another person.

I didn't move, memory filtering back from my dreams. That hadn't happened before; water taking away the flames. I would have remembered. But that wasn't what was strange.

They'd felt like the same thing. The same energy. Yet, for all their terror, the flames also felt somehow faded compared to the water, as if they were only a bad memory. The one side had comforted me and protected me from the other, but suddenly, both seemed familiar.

My heart rate quickened. My gaze crept toward Noah, fright and embarrassment filling me in equal measure.

"You okay?" he asked.

I straightened, my head leaving his shoulder. I looked over, realizing he must have known the moment I was awake.

His brow rose, questioning.

"Yeah," I managed, "I-I think so. But did I try to take any

of your—"

Reassurance filtered through to me, cool and comforting. "No, you're fine. You didn't try to share any magic in your sleep."

My tension remained. If I hadn't taken in any of that, then how else did I explain it? I knew what I'd felt. The water, the flames, all of it.

It'd been Noah.

And when that water had stolen up across my body…

"What is it?" he asked.

I struggled to find the words to explain while fighting to keep myself from blushing. I didn't know if I felt that way about him. He'd showed no sign of feeling that way about me, nor of being aware of what had happened in my dreams. I desperately didn't want to think about it, though. It was bad enough to wonder if he'd picked up anything from me while I slept, let alone risk he'd do so now. "I, um—"

His gaze twitched beyond me and he tensed. I turned. Through the glass doors of the patio, I saw Jace sit up on the couch and look around.

Noah lifted his arm from my shoulders, obviously uncomfortable. "You should probably get inside."

He stood and then extended a hand in silent offer to help me to my feet. He pulled me up, but didn't look at me while he tugged open the door.

Jace froze when we came in. "What—"

The door to Baylie's room opened, cutting him off. She came out and then stopped. "Oh. Wow. You're awake."

Noah shut the patio door behind him and then headed for the kitchen. Baylie glanced between us all warily, and then followed after him.

Jace's brow rose at me. "Ari? What were you—"

"Nothing," I said before he could start in. I strode toward the lump of cushions and blankets that should have been my bed. "We just talked."

I could feel Jace watching me.

"Are you okay?" he asked carefully.

I nodded, bending down to gather my clothes from their folded stack on the floor. "Fine."

Behind me, the air mattress rustled. "Everything alright?" Dhanya asked.

A heartbeat passed before Jace answered. "Yeah."

"Okay…" Dhanya said, clearly not sure she believed him. "You guys sleep well?"

My heart started pounding again. I couldn't deal with this right now. The silent questions—and maybe not-so-silent ones too—would all be bad enough when we drove to see Maia's father.

Tucking my clothes under my arm, I fled toward the bathroom to change.

~ **14** ~

# NOAH

It felt like a minor miracle that Ari's brother hadn't stormed in here after me, though that didn't stop me from waiting for it. I'd seen the look he'd given me the moment he saw Ari come inside with me from the porch. Busying myself with making coffee I wouldn't bother trying to drink, I watched for him from the corner of my eye.

Ari darted across the living room and disappeared into the bathroom.

A moment slid by. Jace appeared in the kitchen archway.

Baylie looked between us. At my glance, she blinked and then retreated past him toward the living room.

I waited.

"Is she alright?" Jace asked like the words were being forced from him.

I paused. I hadn't expected that. Accusations of hurting her, yes. But not that.

"Yeah," I said. "I think so."

His jaw muscles jumped. He looked toward the bathroom.

I studied him. This was making him crazy, I realized. The fact he couldn't do a single thing to help his sister. That beyond the assurances I was certain she was giving him, his only way of knowing if she was okay was to talk to a sentient thunderstorm they'd all been taught to fear.

"She's scared," I told him. "But she's handling it."

He looked back to me, his expression tight. "Is she in pain?"

"No."

Not from anything besides me holding apart that connection between us, anyway.

I kept myself from grimacing. The empathic distance still hurt, but it wasn't excruciating like it'd been that first day. Not even close. Whatever those bastards had done to connect us, it felt like it'd settled. Like maybe I could have broken the link earlier—though I was fairly certain I would have killed Ari in the process—but now it was too strong. It'd grown together, fused like a healing bone.

Which worried me, even if I was grateful it meant the distance wasn't torturing Ari.

"Can you feel what's happening to her?" Jace asked. "What they've done?"

I hesitated. "Yes."

He tensed.

"I don't know what it is, though. Only that it's not anything like me."

He let out a short breath, looking away, but not before I caught the relief that flashed over his face. I couldn't blame him. He seemed to debate whether to say anything more, and then simply gave a short nod and left the kitchen.

I went back to the coffee. In the bathroom, I could feel Ari moving around, a tangled bundle of emotions that were too complex to sort out. I was almost grateful for it, though. I knew she was embarrassed, probably because of the fact she'd let me hold her like that last night. But whatever else she was feeling, it meant she wasn't paying much attention to what was going on inside me.

Not that I really knew either.

I pushed the coffee pot into the machine. I'd wanted to be close to her. I'd wanted to take away her fear and make her believe that somehow this would be alright. I hadn't realized how good it'd been to touch her, not until I couldn't anymore. And I hadn't known what to do when she lay there, this girl who should have been afraid of me, falling asleep in my arms instead.

I hadn't imagined this feeling would come back. Not again.

And I didn't want it to.

I set down the milk and winced when the jug thudded hard against the counter. This wasn't welcome. I couldn't have this in me. I couldn't feel this again, because… because last time hurt. Hell, last time I'd died.

Because everything.

The bathroom door opened. I gritted my teeth, focusing on burying this as best I could. Ari didn't need to know. If there was one shred of privacy left to me, I wanted this to be it.

In my hand, the coffee mug went cold. I muttered a curse.

I felt Baylie walk back in from the living room. I put the

mug down by the sink, not turning around.

"You still drink coffee?" she asked.

"I was making it for you."

"Oh. Thanks." She came over and then paused when she felt how cool it was. From the corner of my eye, I saw her glance to me.

"Sorry."

Baylie hesitated. "That's alright." She turned to the microwave, putting the mug inside.

I closed my eyes. Behind us, I could hear the others packing up. Even if Maia's father wasn't due on the Washington coast for a few days, it'd take us a while to get up there. They wanted to get going as soon as possible.

The microwave started. Baylie returned to my side. "You okay?" she asked me, keeping her voice beneath the low drone of the machine.

I glanced over to see Jace carrying their bags out the door. Ari followed him. "Yeah."

Baylie watched them go. "Noah," she said once the door had closed. "I might not have a connection like you and this girl, but I have something. *And* we're family. What's wrong?"

I grimaced, deeply hoping Ari hadn't picked up on anything. But meanwhile, I couldn't explain. I didn't want this. Talking about it would only make it worse—and harder to ignore. "Nothing."

It didn't take an empathic link to tell she didn't believe me. "Is this about what Ellie—"

"No."

Another moment passed. The microwave beeped. Her mouth tightening, Baylie went and retrieved her coffee.

I looked away. I didn't want to fight. We needed to go, but this wasn't how I wanted to leave things with her after a year of not seeing each other.

Baylie stirred some sweetener into her coffee, the spoon clinking against the mug. "Alright." She set the spoon in the sink. "Well, before you go, I'd still like to talk to you. It's sort of a weird situation. I haven't mentioned it to anybody, but I really need to—"

Icy cold weakness rolled through me, swirling my vision and buckling my knees. My hands caught me on the counter while terror followed, screaming along my connection to Ari.

And then it all vanished.

Shock reverberated in me. She was gone. It was gone. The whole connection was dead.

Oh God, Ari.

"Noah?" Baylie cried.

I exploded outward, racing for the patio door. I heard Baylie yelling for Maia and Dhanya, saw them scrambling up from the couch. I controlled myself enough to keep from shattering the glass door, and then the room was behind me and the apartment was as well.

Jace lay on the ground. The car door was open. I plummeted toward the street.

Ari wasn't inside the SUV.

I rushed upward again, taking in details as fast as possible. I couldn't see her. No cars were racing away; no people were hurrying her off. The early morning sunlight picked out a handful of beachgoers and a smattering of vehicles, but nothing to show a girl who'd just been kidnapped.

Because that's what she was. Kidnapped. Not dead. Just missing.

I raced after the nearest car, darting down to it and then sweeping past. Wind buffered the sedan, enough to make the woman inside grip the wheel harder, though the young boy in the back seat didn't look up from his cell phone. The next car held only a middle-aged man in a suit and no one else. I sped back in the other direction, finding teenagers in sports cars and families on their way to who knew where.

But no Ari.

Panic drummed a rapid beat on my mind while I dashed down street after street, kicking up sand and dust in my wake. She had to be here somewhere. They couldn't just make her disappear.

A familiar presence tugged at me, faint but insistent. Baylie. I rushed back toward the apartment building.

"Noah!" Baylie shouted.

She was standing by the open SUV door. Nearby, Jace seemed to be waking up. I flew down toward them and swiftly returned to human form inside the shelter of the SUV.

"Which way did they go?" I demanded of Jace, bracing myself on the back of the seat.

Jace struggled to reach his feet. Maia and Dhanya helped him. Blood trickled down his neck. In her fingers, Dhanya pinched a yellow-feathered dart like she was afraid it'd bite her.

"Ari," Jace gasped. "Where's Ari?"

"Dammit, which way did they *go*?"

He leaned on the SUV, breathing hard and blinking at the street like he was trying to see.

I swore.

"Noah, stop," Baylie snapped before I could take off. "We have to think."

I stared at her. Think. Right. Of what?

They were going to hurt Ari.

Fury swelled, barely within my control. I should have gone out to the car with her. I shouldn't have left her side.

But how had they *found* us this fast? We hadn't even been in Santa Lucina twenty-four hours; we hadn't been hanging around public places. Hell, I'd stayed out of sight on the porch, just in case anyone drove by.

They shouldn't have found her.

Unless they *had* been tracking her this entire time.

"Your father is a judge," Baylie said, turning to Maia. "Do you know if they have any connections here in town? Any places set up?"

I scowled. They *couldn't* have been tracking Ari. They would have grabbed her before now, and *long* before things became public enough to warrant a car chase through Indiana. For that matter, they wouldn't even have followed Maia and Dhanya in the first place. They'd have just—

Cold realization rushed over me. My gaze darted around the SUV. Maia's SUV, with Maia's license plate. If they'd spotted the SUV…

But out of the whole damn country, how could they have known to look for us *here*?

"I don't think they have anything special in Santa Lucina," Maia said. "But they're really secretive. They wouldn't—"

I gasped, a blur of pain and fear hitting me.

"Ari?" Baylie asked me.

Jace stepped in front of the open car door. "You have to lead us to her."

"Move," I snarled.

Baylie put a hand to Jace's arm. "Do what he says." She looked to me. "We'll follow."

Protests rose in me.

"How?" Jace snapped. "If he—"

"Ari isn't the only one with a connection to Noah," Baylie said. "Now move before he hurts you."

Jace stepped back, staring at her.

"Baylie," I growled.

She glared.

Cursing, I let my human form vanish. My awareness rushed upward and away from them. Ari's presence was hazy, but she was somewhere to the north.

And that was enough.

I raced after her.

# 15

## ARI

Swampy murk surrounded me, thick, cloying, and suffocating. Light and darkness swirled, grayscale and kaleidoscopic. Sludge clogged my ears, deafening me.

Jace. Someone had shot Jace.

I choked, trying to rise.

Things held me down. Lights glared. Shadows were there too, merging together, becoming shapes, becoming people.

Muddled words rose from the muck.

"… should have started…"

"… slower than expected… fighting it."

"… for stage two… force her."

A blur bent toward me. A woman. A needle. Green liquid, glistening.

I struggled, thick noises escaping me. Begging noises. No. No.

The needle entered my arm, sharp and cold.

Warmth spread through me, growing hotter. I twisted, struggling to escape it. Straps held me. I could see them, lashing my arms and legs to the gurney beneath me.

My whole body was starting to burn.

The ground shifted. They were moving me. The lights vanished. Sound echoed strangely, like the walls were far away.

I felt Noah in the distance, coming for me.

The motion ceased and the straps vanished. I shoved at the gurney, fighting to roll the lead weight of my body from it.

Hands grabbed me. Enforcers, their dead eyes barely glancing to me, and the world lurched when they lifted me up. The space around me was dark. A strange glow warped over the walls, coming from a large box of light ahead of me.

They were carrying me toward a tank of water.

I cried out, struggling in their arms. Nothing worked. Their grips were like steel. But they couldn't do this to me. The judges couldn't want to kill me, not after everything else they'd done.

Noah would be here soon. He'd stop this. Any moment now.

Footsteps clunked on metal stairs while the enforcers brought me up to the tank's edge.

"Are you sure? If she dies, we may never have this chance again."

I twisted. A woman, dark-haired, with the ice in her eyes marking her as a judge. It was Irene Marseilles, Logan's mother. She stood on the ground before the tank, Judge Engle at her side. Another man waited next to them; no one I'd ever seen. Monitors with glowing lights and trailing wires surrounded them, watched by the judges' assistants.

I stared. This wasn't happening.

Judge Engle regarded me. "Do it."

The enforcers dropped me into the tank.

Water flooded my mouth. Salt stung my eyes, my nose, my throat. Flailing, I scrambled for the surface.

They were closing something over me.

I fought to swim faster.

A thud echoed through the water. A lid. I ran into it, and there wasn't any space between it and the water. There wasn't any air.

I shoved at the heavy glass. It wouldn't move. They'd locked it closed.

They'd trapped me.

Crying out, I pounded my fist on the glass and my skin shrieked with pain from every impact. My lungs begged for oxygen. Pressure built on my chest like cement blocks crushing me. Blackness clustered around my vision, turning it to a tunnel. Instinct drove my body to try to breathe and water choked me. I coughed and more water poured in. I fell away from the lid.

Salt burned in my eyes. Burned all over me. Everything was burning.

I was burning.

Noah would come for me.

I hit the bottom of the tank. My body spasmed. I gasped and then choked on another lungful of water. My eyes widened. The world grew sharp. Painful. Bright.

He'd get here soon.

Another spasm rocked me. My arms were changing.

I stared. Green stains rushed down my arms, down the backs of my hands and out to my fingers. Pressure crushed down on my body. The heat increased. I thrashed, fighting to escape the agony.

My clothes were burning.

My legs were melting. Stretching. Fusing.

I screamed.

Poison ripped through me, tangled around me, and wrapped my body in glowing threads of emerald light. My clothes turned to dust and my legs were devoured by the magic. Spikes grew from the backs of my arms, long and translucent. My back arched from the bottom of the tank while my hands beat on the glass floor, desperate to break through.

Pain rose higher like a screeching crescendo.

And died.

I collapsed to the ground. Ragged breaths entered my lungs in frantic gasps. And then my brow furrowed. I was underwater. I was breathing. I…

My gaze moved to my body.

I choked. My legs were gone and what remained wasn't human. Wasn't dehaian. Wasn't anything I'd ever seen.

My gaze turned to the side.

Judge Engle watched me. His lip curled.

"Excellent."

## ∽ 16 ∼

## NOAH

Ari's presence swirled in my head, murky and confused.

I tore after it. She was close. She was scared.

She was calling my name.

I sped toward a stretch of warehouses at the edge of town. Barbed wire surrounded the complex and trucks rolled past the gates like everything was business as usual. Workers called to one another and forklifts drove by them, carrying boxes and barrels on wood pallets.

She was in the large building at the farthest edge of the lot. The one without any workers or machinery around it. The one with security cameras on the walls like tiny black gargoyles.

The one with a sedan outside, a sedan I could *swear* I'd seen driving down the street near Baylie's apartment, now sitting next to the warehouse with its trunk open.

Ari's fear pounded harder at my mind. I couldn't think with it beating at me. Going down there in human form was out, though. It had been anyway. And the judges probably already knew I was here. They must have planned this. They'd most likely been tracking me from the moment they took her.

Her fear spiked higher, and agony followed. Intense, unspeakable agony. They were torturing her. Oh my God, they were *killing* her.

Ari screamed inside my mind.

I charged at the warehouse. The enormous garage door shredded and flew inward. A bright box was at the opposite end of the cavernous space and I raced toward it, horrified. Ari was inside. But not Ari. They'd—

Pain ripped through me. The world turned to white light. All of me burned. I flung myself backward, trying to escape it.

Another wall of light met me and the agony returned. I twisted away.

The pain lessened.

I froze, hovering invisibly while perceptions hit me from every side. Magic glowed from steel girders all around me. Light rippled between them like the translucent walls of a massive, warehouse-sized box. That judge from the mansion stood beyond the far end of them, a woman and a dark-haired man at his side. Machines waited behind them, beeping and buzzing. By the gaping opening in the warehouse, men in black suits rolled down another garage door, sealing the room like they'd known I'd break past the original door all along.

And Ari…

A shudder ran through me. They'd changed her. She lay on the bottom of a brightly lit tank of water. Her legs had become a tail, but not like any I'd seen on a dehaian. Long and sinuous like an eel, it was fringed with a rippling and translucent fin of pale gold. Her scales were dark green like the poison that had spread through Maia, but brushed with gold of their own. The scaling ran over her stomach and chest, greener toward the center and darker toward her sides. On her arms, the coloring continued though the scales didn't, the emerald tone twisting along her bare skin like a watercolor stain. Her ears were pointed now, and edged by frills of gold as well. Spikes stood out from her forearms—the most dehaian thing on her—while green and gold stained her temples and the hollows of her cheeks like a ghost of scaling there too.

And her eyes…

They weren't human. The whites and the irises had gone utterly yellow-green. A black, vertical slit cut through them and on anyone else, they would have looked like the eyes of a snake.

But they were just *her*. Inhuman or not, I could see her fear in them. I didn't even need our connection to read her terror.

The judge walked between us, his gaze scanning the translucent magic holding me.

"We know you're in there," he said calmly. "Show yourself."

Fury rippled through me. I flew at the walls.

Pain erupted in a blinding flash. I heard Ari scream.

I retreated. On the bottom of the tank, she was curled into a ball, gasping and shaking.

Sorrow flooded me. I hadn't meant—

Trembling reassurance came back to me from Ari. She knew.

The judge glanced to her and then returned his gaze to the cage. "We've had centuries to plan how we would find you and kill you, Beast, and we learned from your escape in Maine. We had this enclosure specifically designed in case we were so fortunate as to locate you in your mistress' favorite town. Thankfully, you returned here, which means we have the chance to use it. This cage *far* exceeds the last one, however, and it comes with several improvements. Now show yourself, lest we use them."

I shuddered with rage. There had to be a way out of this. Something that wouldn't kill us both.

The judge looked to a petite, blonde woman by the machines.

Magic roared from the walls, howling through me for less than a heartbeat, and then it vanished.

Everything in me felt burned. I wasn't sure how much of that I could take, or how much Ari could stand either. On the bottom of the tank, she whimpered, agony echoing from her.

"Now," the judge ordered. "Or we do that again."

I watched Ari for a moment. My awareness condensed, drawing into human form.

The judge's eyebrow twitched up at the sight of me. "Young," he commented. "An interesting choice, though I suppose it *was* your teenage mistress who chose your form."

Contempt showed on his face. He turned back toward the people by the machines. "Is the siphoning system ready?"

One of them nodded. "Yes, Judge Engle."

"Good. Prepare for stage three."

They started toward Ari.

"Get away from her!" I shouted.

Judge Engle looked back at me, his eyebrow twitching higher like I'd performed a particularly interesting trick. He held up a hand. The people heading for Ari stopped.

"Compassion?" the judge asked. "Or self-preservation? I'm curious: how *human* did your mistress command you to be?"

I shuddered.

"Kill the girl," he ordered his people.

I lunged forward.

"Stop," he commanded.

The people moving toward Ari froze. I staggered back from the barrier, my body shaking from residual pain.

"Judge Marseilles, are you seeing this?" he asked.

He glanced over when the woman joined him, her eyes as cold as his. The dark-haired man sauntered after them and something in the way he moved seemed wrong. Off. I couldn't put my finger on it.

"Indeed," Judge Marseilles replied. "It appears you were right. The dehaian girl did alter more than the Beast's appearance when she took command of the creature."

"What is the benefit, I wonder?"

"An overlay, perhaps? Control through emotions? Magic failed them, you will remember."

"True. But how *foolish*. Its behavior has become so erratic that it *interceded* on behalf of the subject—" Judge Engle's head twitched back toward Ari. "—rather than assist in an apparent dehaian offensive as we assumed it would. Surely even the dehaians would realize that level of autonomy is not in their best interest?"

The woman's brow shrugged as if she couldn't explain it. "Either way, it served our purpose, so does it matter?"

Judge Engle turned away, shaking his head. "I suppose not." He glanced to the blonde woman by the machines again. "Have the scans on the girl returned?"

The blonde looked like she was made of ice, rigid to the point of cracking but totally cold. "Yes, sir." Her eyes skirted toward me and then darted away. "She can be processed at any time."

He nodded. "Good. Drain and store a sufficient supply of energy from the creature in case the girl requires assistance before she can be introduced to the open water."

Lightning shot down at me from the girders above, the electricity green and white with magic.

I shouted, my legs collapsing beneath me when it struck. Magic tore through me as if shredding the core of what I was and dragging it away. My body vanished, but the pain was worse. I crumpled back into human form, crying out from the agony.

The lightning stopped.

"What's wrong?" Judge Engle asked the blonde.

"Nothing, sir. We're finished."

His brow twitched up. "Already?" His cold gaze ran across me. "How much power did your original masters give you?"

He shook his head as if dismissing the thought. "Well, in that case, commence processing, but do not destroy the creature till the procedure is complete. I want to be certain the girl is fully ready before we begin the next stage of our offensive on Yvaria."

Alarm shot through me. "What?"

Judge Engle glanced back to me. "Your masters declared war on us, Beast. Surely you remember, seeing as you were there?"

There was something weird in his voice. Some sick form of amusement.

"Dehaians aren't my *masters*," I snapped. "And Yvaria didn't do anything."

His amusement didn't fade.

"Three minutes, sir," the blonde woman said.

"Excellent." He turned to the other judge. "It would be interesting to see if her brother responds as well to alteration into a strakirin as she has done."

Judge Marseilles nodded. "I agree. With such close genetics to the primary, he would be an interesting candidate for post-adjustment testing."

They focused their attention on the nearest monitor while around the room, the others began fine-tuning the machines.

"Hey!" I shouted at the judges. "No one declared anything! You—"

"They know."

My gaze snapped over. The dark-haired man hadn't turned aside with the others. A smirk twisted his lip, condescending and cruel. Running his gaze over me like he was studying a bug, he sauntered closer to the cage.

I stared at him, the oddness of his motions suddenly clicking. Dehaian. He was a dehaian. I'd bet on it.

The man's brow rose. "What is it, Beast?"

"What are you?" I demanded. "Yvarian? From some other nation?"

His smile grew.

"Helpful," Judge Marseilles commented lightly. "That's what he is. It's been quite enlightening, having him around. Not only did our friend and his associates provide us with a supposed dehaian massacre around which to rally the ruanir, but he's also given us a wealth of information on your mistress and her people."

"You stay away from her," I ordered.

The dehaian man laughed. "You have no idea what's coming, do you, Beast? What the strakirin will do to your precious Yvarian mistress and anyone else who sides with her. What this girl will become." He turned his attention to Ari. "You're ancient, my dear. So new and so old, all at the same time. Or you will be."

"What the hell does that mean?" I demanded.

"Just that it's been an inspiration, working with the Judiciary," the dehaian said. "They're so… *committed*. It's been a pleasure to see that after all this time. And their people…" Humor showed on his face. "Sure, there are a few out there causing trouble and whatnot, but the majority? Like frenzied bottom-feeders, waiting for the food to drop." He chuckled, looking to Ari again. "Your mother was most agreeable, did you know? She volunteered her own daughter, simply to receive the judges' favor. She fed you drugs and mixtures for a year, all so that you would be primed to absorb the Beast's magic that night at your little 'party'—or as I think she considered it, the time she'd finally be free of you."

His grin widened. "The judges *have* been tracking you,

Beast. They knew you'd be there, knew you'd see the dehaians coming out of the ocean. They figured you'd side with us; kill the ruanir simply because you saw us doing so. They'd already made certain the girl couldn't have stopped herself from taking in your magic if she tried; even being *near* you was enough to start the reaction." He glanced to Ari. "It hurt, didn't it? Being near him. Yet no one else reacted like that. Didn't that seem odd?"

He shook his head, amused, and turned his attention to me. "Bottom-feeders, I swear. But it would have been brilliant. The judges would have rushed her away from the bloodbath, treating her for 'ocean magic poisoning'—" He chuckled like he'd told a joke. "—all so they could finish making her into what she'd already been selected to become. After all, they've had their eye on her for a *long* time."

Ari stared at him, shock and pain pounding through her. "What?" she breathed, her voice carrying from speakers on the sides of the tank.

"Enough," Judge Engle interrupted. "Are we ready?"

The blonde gave a tight nod. "Yes, sir."

"No, wait," Ari begged the judges. "Please, you don't have to—"

"Miss Moreau," Judge Engle sighed, "this is unnecessary and will only serve to prolong your procedure. As our friend said, we have been preparing you for this since the start and you will be fully accepting of your enhancement once it is done. Thus voluntary submission is best and will afford you the least pain during the transition."

He motioned to the enforcers beside the tank. They turned to the machines there.

Ari's fear spiked higher. Twisting in the water, she scrambled up from the bottom of the tank and slammed into the lid as if trying to break the lock holding it closed. "No! Don't make me like them!"

Horror shot through me. I shoved away from the ground. I could barely stand. My body shook with agony and the feeling that the life had been dragged out of me.

The enforcer flipped a switch on the machine.

Magic lit the walls of the tank around Ari. She screamed, her hands going to her head and her body thrashing. Pain roared through the connection between us, driving me back to the ground.

Her presence in my mind shuddered. Flashed cold like it had suddenly frozen, only to flare hot again.

"Ari!" I shouted. I staggered to my feet again. I wouldn't let them do this. I wouldn't let them kill her and leave her body alive.

Agony surged through her, sending her tail crashing into the walls as she fought to escape it.

The cold-hot feeling came again. She lurched, her yellow-green eyes locking on me, wide with horror. "Noah…"

She screamed again.

My gaze went to the barrier. They were destroying her. Breaking free might destroy me.

I didn't care.

I gave in to the rage of the Beast.

❦ 17 ❦

## ARI

The world was crumbling and I couldn't make it stop.

Pain shot through me, transforming to brittle ice in my mind before cracking and burning me again. And the pulses of it were coming faster. They clawed into me, freezing and bleeding everything inside me. At their touch, it felt like parts of me died.

And something dark slithered into the deadened space. Something cold, sinking into me like a black stain.

It hurt. Everything hurt. I didn't know what they were killing anymore. What I was fighting to save or why. I wanted this to stop. *All* of this to stop. I didn't want to hurt anymore and I—

Rage exploded through my mind.

In a white-hot wave, it surged through me. The cold and the pain shredded before it, disintegrating like tissue paper in the face of a nuclear blast. My eyes flew open.

Noah had become a nightmare. Black clouds erupted from where he'd stood, billowing outward to fill the enormous cage.

Lightning flashed inside them, illuminating the churning storm with shades of blood red and bruised purple by turns. The judges shouted, running for their machines.

"Get the girl out of here!" Judge Engle yelled at the enforcers.

They scrambled up the steps toward the top of the tank.

The storm crashed into the translucent walls on every side and pain shrieked through me at the impact. Noah thrashed against them, lightning snarling from within him to strike the barriers.

And the walls began to falter.

Judge Engle slammed his hand down on one of the machines.

The barriers turned to white light.

Pain blasted through me. Magic ripped into him from all sides, draining him and devouring him. He pressed hard against the barriers, fighting to break them down.

It wasn't enough.

He was dying.

They were killing him.

I was going to feel Noah die.

Lightning erupted from me.

The walls of the tank shattered. Water gushed into the room. Electricity lashed out of me, tearing down the enforcers and crawling over the machines. The barriers around Noah collapsed.

Black clouds rushed from the cage, ripping past the judges and the assistants and surging toward me. In a heartbeat, they engulfed me. People screamed. The ground disappeared. A crash roared around me, like the world was coming down.

But I couldn't breathe. The water was gone. Air seared my skin.

And the wind shifted. Swept down.

I plunged into water again.

The pain faded. The sensation of rushing motion slowed. Darkness surrounded me. Cool water swirled over me, as if checking frantically to see if I was alright.

And then it solidified into hands on my face. The darkness faded, drawing in and becoming Noah again. He stared at me in the deep blue twilight.

"Are you okay?" he asked anxiously.

I didn't know how to respond. I could hear him clearly, but we were underwater again. The thing that my legs had become was rippling slowly, holding me in place, while the edges of the translucent fin around it glowed with a strange bioluminescence. From the corner of my eye, I could see my hair floating in the water, all of it glistening with golden light as well. My skin shimmered green and gold in the darkness and the spikes were pulling back into my forearms like they'd never existed at all.

And my mind felt shattered. Broken, like someone had gone at it with a sledgehammer. The jagged edges cut me, too painful to come near.

I choked on a sob.

He drew me into his arms. My fingers dug into his back and I buried my face in his shoulder.

"Shh," he whispered.

I held onto him tighter, crying while he ran a hand over my

hair and murmured comfort. Sympathy and care poured into me, cool and gentle and taking the sting of the damage done by the judges away. My tears slowed.

"Are *you* okay?" I asked quietly, not leaving his arms.

Another wave of compassion came from him. "Yeah, I'll be alright."

I drew a breath, relieved.

"I know a place I can take you," he said. "A place down here where you'll be safe from them."

Alarm made me pull back so that I could see him better. "What? No. Noah, I can't—"

"They're going to come after you, Ari. You heard them. They have all these plans for you and they have dehaians working with them. They're not going to let you go."

I turned away, searching for a response. "B-but I can't stay like *this*, Noah. I mean, *look* at me. I—"

"You don't have to. But until we can stop whatever it is they're after and make sure you're safe, it'd be better—"

"*Please.*" Frantic desperation pushed at me. "I want to change back. To see if I can change back like the dehaians do. I know I'm not like them, but if I have that same ability…" I choked on a breath. "I have to try. I can't just stay like this and not know if I'll ever be human again."

He grimaced, looking away.

"What if the effects build over time?" I argued urgently. "What if the longer I stay like this, the less chance I'll have of ever going back?" Tears strangled me, driven by fear. "*Please*, Noah. I'm begging you. Please."

He closed his eyes, nodding. "Alright." His hand moved down to mine. "Can you swim?"

I couldn't quite bring myself to look down at the thing that had been my legs, but at a thought, it rippled and propelled me forward. I cringed at the feeling.

"Come on," he said.

He led me upward, his body moving through the water without any effort at all, like the ocean itself was adjusting for him. Like he was flying.

The blue twilight grew brighter. "How deep were we?" I asked faintly.

He hesitated. "Deep enough."

I shivered.

We continued on, climbing higher through the water. Waves rushed overhead, sending quivers of fear through me at how wrong it was to be under them and breathing. Ocean magic surrounded me and there wasn't a hope of keeping it out. I felt it coursing through me, unchecked and powerful and terrifying. At my side, I knew Noah felt it too. He seemed stronger with every moment, as if he was rebuilding within himself everything the judges had tried to take.

I wished I could do the same.

The seafloor appeared past the murk, drawing closer the farther we swam. The waves tumbled toward shore above us, and only a short distance separated them from the seafloor.

Noah slowed.

I watched him, anxiety jittering through me.

"Ready?" he asked.

I nodded.

He rose up and pulled me with him from the water.

Pain seared my skin like the air was acid. My lungs choked on oxygen too thick to breathe. Light burned my eyes and I twisted in his arms, trying to flee back toward the water.

Noah didn't let me go. I cried out, thrashing. Everything hurt. I couldn't do it. I couldn't escape this.

His arms tightened on me. Images flashed in my mind. A beach. Another girl. Another time. His arms around her while she screamed and cried in the water.

Magic rippled through me. The tail split. My legs returned.

My lungs gasped in air and my eyes flew open. My skin rushed back. The green scales faded.

Mortification hit me. I was naked in his arms.

Noah didn't move, his face turned to the side. "Dehaians can do swimsuits," he said, his voice tightly controlled. "Concentrate on the scales becoming that."

I focused with all my might.

Scales formed over me again, like a green and gold one-piece. I remembered how to breathe.

Noah relaxed a bit. His hands loosened on me, but even against the swimsuit, they felt like they were touching my skin. I blushed, dropping my gaze to the water and trying to bury the not-entirely-unpleasant chills that rushed through me at the sensation.

He felt them anyway. Tension shot through him and, just for a heartbeat, something flashed by the connection between us, almost like a desire to feel my reaction again.

And then it vanished as if it'd never been.

He let me go. Trying to balance on my unsteady legs, I looked up at him. He didn't meet my eyes, and if such a thing as stone walls existed between us anymore, it felt like he was putting them up now.

I wasn't certain what to say. "Thank you for coming to rescue me."

He hesitated, and then managed a nod.

The water rushed into shore around us.

"We should get out of sight," he said. "Figure out what to do next."

I nodded.

Still not looking at me, he started out of the water. Sand and rocks shifted beneath my feet as I followed him, while the tide pushed and tugged at me as if it couldn't decide whether to drive me to shore or drag me back out to sea. Ahead of us, a small stretch of beach waited, all of it covered in boulders, gravel, and sparse plant-life.

An SUV pulled to a stop on the road beyond the beach. Relief rushed through Noah.

I looked to him. "Who are they?"

Noah froze. Fear crept through me at the terrible, horror-struck feeling that shivered out from him.

"What?" he whispered.

My fear grew stronger, bubbling toward panic. I trembled, my lungs fighting to breathe against it. "Noah… who are they?"

His head turned toward me. "Your family."

The trembling became stronger. My gaze returned to the

guy and girls hurrying from the SUV. I didn't recognize them. Not a one of them. There wasn't anything in my memory about them at all.

A gasp escaped me. My mouth worked, trying to find words or a cry, I couldn't be sure.

Noah took my arm. I looked to him again.

"We will fix this," he said, his voice intense. "I *promise* you. Maia's father is a judge. We will *make* him make this right."

I had no idea who he meant.

His hand tightened on me. "I promise," he repeated.

I clung to the word while I trailed him to the shore.

A pale-skinned girl with dark hair raced toward us, an olive-skinned girl chasing after her. A guy with golden-brown hair rushed around from the driver's side, while a blonde girl stayed by the passenger door, staring at me in alarm.

"Are you okay?" the dark-haired girl cried. "What's that on you?"

My gaze went to Noah, terrified and questioning. He was looking toward the blonde, and at her incredulous glance, he shook his head quickly.

"Just something they put her in," Noah said.

"What did they do?" the guy demanded. "Are you alright?"

"We need to go," Noah cut in before they could keep questioning. "The judges will be after her."

The guy hesitated and then nodded. The dark-haired girl motioned as if to urge me back toward the SUV.

I glanced to Noah.

A wave of that same, shivering determination came from

him. The one that promised this would change. That we'd fix this.

That I wouldn't be this way forever.

I nodded. Surrounded by strangers, I walked toward the SUV.

# AFTERWORD

## The Awakened Fate Series will continue!

Join Skye Malone's mailing list to hear about new releases!

www.skyemalone.com/mailinglist

## Love the book?

Please leave a review on Amazon, Goodreads, or your favorite book-related website!

## Other titles by Skye Malone

The Awakened Fate Series

The Demon Guardians Series

The Kindling Trilogy

## About Skye Malone

Skye Malone is a fantasy and paranormal romance author, which means she spends most of her time not-quite-convinced that the magical things she imagines couldn't actually exist.

A Midwestern girl who migrated to the Pacific Northwest, she dreams someday of traveling the world – though in the meantime she'll take any story that whisks her off to a place where the fantastic lives inside the everyday. She loves strong and passionate characters, complex villains, and satisfying endings that stay with you long after the book is done. An inveterate writer, she can't go a day without getting her hands on a keyboard, and can usually be found typing away while she listens to all the adventures unfolding in her head.

### Connect with Skye Malone

Website: www.skyemalone.com
Twitter: www.twitter.com/Skye_Malone
Facebook: www.facebook.com/authorskyemalone
Instagram: www.instagram.com/authorskyemalone